BIG BALLER

COCKY HERO CLUB PRODUCTION

KATRINA MARIE

Big Baller is a standalone story inspired by Vi Keeland and Penelope Ward's Playboy Pilot. It's published as part of the Cocky Hero Club world, a series of original works, written by various authors, and inspired by Keeland and Ward's *New York Times* bestselling series.

ONE

Bentley

TODAY IS THE DAY. The first game of the season, and if all goes well, I'll be appearing on the court as an Austin Rattler. This moment is what I've been working my entire life toward. Being a starter for Hilltown University can never compare to today. Being picked up by a professional team out of college is slim, but I was able to lead my team to win huge national championships. That brought the attention of professional teams. Even better, I was signed on by the one in my city. It's a win no matter what way you look at it.

A groan comes from the other side of my bed. Shit. I totally forgot she was here. This is why I never let the women I bring home stay overnight. Hell, I probably should have gotten a room for the night. The only reason she's in my bed is because I'm a basketball player. She's chasing her way to fame. My teammates warned me about girls like her, but there's no reason for me to be worried. No, I don't do relationships. A bit of fun here and there is fine. There's zero chance of me putting a ring on anyone's finger. Not after my dad bailed on my mom. Bailed on me and Gabby. I've seen what relationships do to those they leave behind. I refuse to let that happen to me. The single life works out wonderfully for me.

"What time is it?" Mary, or is it Marnie, says from beneath the comforter. Her voice is gravelly and sleepy.

"Almost nine," I say. "We should probably get you home."

She throws the comforter down, breasts exposed, and I remember why I brought her home last night. "Seriously," she asks. "You're just going to send me on my merry little way."

I slide out of bed, grab my boxers from the floor, and push my legs through them. "I have things I need to do today." Like get some practice rounds in before the game tonight. I want Coach to know that I'm capable of starting. That I'm more than just a bench rider.

"Then what was the point of bringing me over?"

"Look." I do my best to keep my eyes on her face and not let myself be tempted by her gorgeous body. "We both wanted the same thing last night. You said you weren't looking for a relationship, and neither am I. What exactly were you expecting?"

"Breakfast would have been nice," she grumbles as she throws the rest of the blanket off of her. She storms to the bathroom and seconds later I hear water running.

All right then, I guess she's going to take a shower before she leaves. She rode with me in my car, and with her attitude, I think it'd be best if I'm not the person to take her home. Thank God Uber and Lyft exist. Otherwise, I'd be dealing with her angry grumbles.

I grab my phone off the dresser and head toward the

bathroom. My knuckles tap lightly on the door three times and there's no response. I crack the door open just enough for her to hear me. "Hey," damn it, I forgot to ask what her name is. I need to create a note in my phone so I'll have a way to check without sounding like a complete asshole. "What's your address? I will get you a ride home."

"Don't worry about it," she deadpans. "I already have a ride." Her voice is ice in the steamy bathroom and I know she won't be someone I see again. I'll be lucky if she doesn't run my name through the mud. It won't matter, though. She knew exactly what last night was about, even if she wants to act like it was supposed to be so much more.

"Um, okay." Uncertainty about what I'm supposed to respond with flows through me. I'm not one that gets flustered easily. I've always had to be a grownup. My mom may have wanted me to stay little, but that's not possible when she worked so much and me and my sister were left at home to fend for ourselves most days. "I'll be downstairs."

Mary/Marnie wants breakfast and maybe if I have something ready for her ride home, she'll be in a better mood. Food makes me happy, and I assume it does for everyone else. I walk down the stairs and the blank walls on either side make me wish I had pictures I could hang there. Something to make it seem less sterile. Mom's house is full of pictures and mementos. There's barely a square inch that isn't covered with mine or my sister's smiling faces, or awards and medals we've won. I could put up some shots the photographers at Hilltown took during my last season there, but that may appear a bit pretentious. Don't get me wrong, I'm a badass on the court, otherwise I wouldn't be playing professionally. But...I don't want to come home and see pictures of myself. Even I would get sick of that.

The kitchen is filled with sunshine as I round the

corner to see what I might have to feed my overnight guest. Floor to ceiling windows take up one wall, and I squint my eyes waiting for them to adjust. Living here is an upgrade from the shitty apartment I lived in with a few of my team-mates in college. It's weird being on my own and I'm not sure how I feel about it. The privacy is nice, but other than that? It can get lonely. Hence the pissed off woman in my shower. I really need to figure out her name before she's even more furious and tries to come up with something for blackmail.

I pull the fridge door open, and there's nothing in there. I'm not sure why I expected a plethora of food for the taking. If I don't grab food with my teammates, I'm usually at my mom's eating her food. I'm a horrible cook and if I didn't have to keep my performance up on the court, I'd live off of frozen food. Ah, I should check the freezer, I'm bound to have some frozen breakfast in there.

I yank the door open and there are exactly two breakfast burritos on the top shelf. It's probably not what she wanted when she said breakfast would be nice, but it's better than nothing. Throwing them in the microwave, I lean against the counter. This has to win me some brownie points. At least enough that she won't be too pissed about essentially being thrown out.

The microwave beeps and I pull out some paper plates while the food cools down. As I'm setting the food on the plates, I hear the click clack of her heels tapping down the stairs. She must be done with her shower. She's definitely taking her sweet time coming down the stairs. There's no noise for a few seconds, as if she's determining what her exit strategy should be, but then her heels pick up the beat and she's standing a few feet in front of the stairs wearing her clothes from last night.

Picking up one plate, I hold it out as an offering. Like I'm a good pup that's done a great deed. "I made breakfast."

She scrunches up her nose in disgust. "That's what you call breakfast?" She shakes her head and walks toward the front door. "My ride's here. I would say it's been fun but..." She lets the sentence trail off.

"Marnie, wait." Yes, that's her name. She didn't recoil at the sound of it, so I must have gotten it right. "You can take it with you."

"I'm good," she calls over her shoulder. She's out of the house before I make it to her.

Well, I guess that takes care of that problem. I hope to hell she didn't use all the hot water. I need to get ready to head to the stadium.

This is it. The first of many games to happen on this court. I used to dream about this moment when I was little and here I am. My feet jogging across the shiny hardwood floor. My hands shooting the ball toward the goal I never thought I'd be tall enough to reach. This is what I've worked for my entire life. And tonight, I will prove how valuable I am to the team.

Coach calls the team over to the bench. The game is about to start and I'm itching to be back out there. "All right guys, I know it's only preseason, but we need to start the season off with a win. Go out there and take care of the ball." He goes over a few plays with us and calls out the starting line.

I bounce on my toes, hoping he'll call my name, but he doesn't. My shoulders sag and I make my way to one of the empty chairs along the sideline. I choose one closer to the coach rather than at the very end. I doubt it'll have any impact on him deciding to play me, but maybe if I show some initiative, he'll give me a shot.

Halfway through the game and I'm still riding the bench. We're up by fifteen points, and the other team is getting mad. I have a feeling they will come back fiercely for the second half. I wish I was out there playing my heart out. I know I'm just a rookie, but how am I supposed to prove myself if he only lets me on the hardwood during practice. Practice isn't what I'm here for. I'm here to make a name for myself, to take another team to the championships. That's the problem, though. I'm not leading a team anymore. I'm the new guy, the one that has to earn their way to start. I did it in high school, then again in college. I'll do it this time, too. One day these fans will be screaming my name.

TWO

Jolene

THERE ARE days that I wish I could call in sick. This is one of them. I groan as I roll across my bed and turn off the alarm blaring in the quiet morning. It's still dark outside and if I didn't absolutely need my job, I wouldn't be going in.

This is the first time in a few weeks that I've been able to sleep in my own bed. Laying in my own bed with my own pillows is so much better than the crappy hotels with the loud noises of the adjacent rooms. It's the life I chose when I applied to be a flight attendant at International Airlines, much to my parent's dismay. They wanted me to do the normal thing. Go to college. Find a steady job, then a husband, and start a family.

It's not that I'm against any of those things, but when you grow up in a small town, the first thing you want to do is leave. I wanted to spread my wings and explore the world. Being a flight attendant helps me fulfill that dream. The exhilaration of not knowing where you're going until the week before is everything. Meeting new people, experiencing new things. I'm living my best life. Well, mostly.

I need to stop lying around and get ready. It's a good thing I always have my bag packed. The plane won't wait for me. I just hope Lana is working with me on this trip. She has a way of keeping me distracted when *he* is the one flying. Carter Clines broke my heart and though he's with someone else, someone he loves and cares about. It still stings. Before Kendall, I lasted two months with the pilot. That's the longest he had ever been with anyone. I thought that meant I was special. Turns out, I was just another woman in a long line of women before me.

I can't think about him right now, even if I will see him in a few short hours. Well, more like hear him. This is another international flight, and that means he'll be singing to all the passengers. Making sure there are headphones in my bag is a must. It'll give me something to listen to while blocking him out. It's not that I'm bitter or anything. I'm happy for him. He's found "the one". But that doesn't lessen the sting of rejection. Especially when I thought we were going somewhere. And...that's the last bit of attention I'm going to give Triple C. For now, anyway.

Rolling out of bed, I groan. "Goodbye, sweet and comfortable bed," I pat the bed as if it were my pet. "Until we meet again." Dramatic? Maybe. Do I care? Not even a little bit. A person never really appreciates the small things until they're sleeping on a rock-hard mattress to the tune of banging headboards on the other side of the wall. Not all places are like that, thank God. But the ones that are, I never get a good night's rest.

A quick shower is all I have time for. I hurry to my small bathroom and turn on the water, not even letting it completely warm up before I jump in. That extra time in bed I spent agonizing over working with Carter cost me precious minutes. I don't have the luxury of letting it get hot before I wash my hair and body. I'm in and out in less than five minutes. The steam hasn't even had the chance to build up in the tiny space. Next time, I will not drag ass when the alarm goes off.

Still in my robe, I grab my phone off the nightstand and perch on the edge of my bed while I blow-dry my hair. Normally I'd do this in the bathroom, but I'm not ready to say bye to the bed. The low hum of the blow dryer is my soundtrack as I check social media and email. It's all mostly junk, and I don't know why I even bother. A message from Lana pops up on the screen and I hope that means she'll be flying with me today.

Lana: How long until you get to the airport?
Jolene: I don't know. Thirty, maybe forty-five minutes.
Lana: Why so long? I need someone to bitch to about my long horrendous night.
Jolene: I still need to put my makeup on. What happened?
Lana: Put it on here. And nothing too bad. Just douchy guys at the hotel bar.
Jolene: Why didn't you tell me you were staying here overnight? You could have stayed here.
Lana: It was late when I got in. And I didn't want to chance waking you up. I know how much you love to sleep when you're actually home.
Jolene: I'm almost done blow drying my hair.

I'll use the makeup in my suitcase and put it on while you fill me in on the guys.
Lana: See you in a few. Be careful.
Jolene: Always. And I'll be catching a cab. As long as they get me there in one piece, I'll be happy.

It's a relief she'll be on the same plane as me. At least, I think she will be. She never said we had the same schedule. Things between us have been strained for a while. After I started messing around with Carter, I almost cost us our friendship. But we're working past that. We'll be back at best friend status before I know it. Hell, she didn't even give me a mocking "I told you so" when he broke things off. I can't believe I almost let a guy come between us. Especially one that had zero intentions of making us a permanent thing.

Turning the blow dryer off, I unplug it and toss it on my bed. I keep an extra, smaller one, in my suitcase so I won't need it. I pull a brush through my hair a couple of times, and toss some clothes on. I should change into my uniform, but there will be time for that at the airport. Lana needs to vent. Listening to her is the least I can do after all the crap I caused between us.

I grab the bag that holds my uniforms and my suitcase. We'll only be gone for a few days, but something feels different about this trip. And it has nothing to do with the hot pilot all the women swoon over. With nothing left to do, I walk out of the apartment and lock up. I should have called a cab as soon as I told Lana I'd be there early. Luckily, I live downtown and there's sure to be a cab driving through to the airport.

～

Lana is sitting outside the gate when I walk up. She grins as soon as she sees me. "It's about time you got here."

"I told you it'd take me a bit." I set the bag holding my uniforms across a couple seats and wrap my arms around Lana's shoulders. "I forgot to call a cab before I left and had to wait until one passed by." Letting go of her, I take a step back. "You'd think I'd be used to sharing a small space with someone I don't know. But, no. The person I ended up in the cab with was awful."

"More awful than asshole guys at a bar?" She sits down and pats the seat next to her.

"I think so." The small plastic seat is cold against my thin leggings, and a shiver courses through me. "He was picking his nose behind his hand and then wiping it on the side of the seat. It was disgusting." I've seen some crazy things while working as a flight attendant, but I don't think anything beats what I witnessed. It's way too early in the morning to deal with that nonsense.

"You might have me beat, girl." She turns until she's facing me and slides one leg under her butt.

"What happened last night?"

"Nothing outside of the usual," Lana waves me off. "You know how some people get when they find out you're a flight attendant. The mile-high jokes come out in droves."

"That sucks." Groaning, I reach into my suitcase and grab my makeup bag. I don't wear as much as I do when I go out, like that happens very much, but I need to look presentable. "That, my friend, is why I've stopped going to the hotel bars after flights."

"Whatever," she laughs. "You don't go out because

you're worried you're going to run into a certain pilot. You need to get over that. He's moved on, and so should you."

She's right. He's the reason I don't go out much anymore. It's not even that it hurts that much. It's the awkwardness that I know will permeate the air. How can you casually be around someone you've screwed and things not be weird? "I have moved on."

"Then who are you seeing?"

"You know damn well how hard it is to start and maintain a relationship in our line of work."

"True story." She pushes her foot back to the floor and sits up straight. That's her serious expression. Nothing good is going to come out of that. I keep hoping the low murmur surrounding us will drown out whatever she's about to say. Not even a baby cries to distract her. "Speaking of work..."

"This better not be some way for you to rub in the fact that we're flying with Carter as the pilot today."

"It's not. I swear." Lana makes an x over her heart and holds out her pinky, waiting for me to take it. She's resorting to child-like promises and I know she will not tease me.

I hook my finger in hers, "Okay, spill."

"We're sort of being put on a new assignment after this flight."

"What do you mean?"

I watch people get up and stand in line to board their planes. The voice over the speakers calling for passengers to board and head off on their own adventures. Lana waits for them to quiet down before continuing. "Apparently, International Airlines is also going to work with basketball teams."

"Huh." What does that have to do with us? "Are they sponsoring them or something?"

"Nope," she pops the p before adding, "we are their

transportation. They don't always travel together from what I hear, but most of the flights we'll be on will be shorter." She pauses, hoping I'll give her a reaction. "And they'll include super-hot athletes. Ones I'm sure will be just fine with a night or two of fun."

"Of course, that would catch your attention," I roll my eyes. I swear this woman will never settle down. If that's what she wants, who am I to tell her differently? "Why us?"

"No idea." She shrugs and people watches. "But I'm not complaining. It'll be nice to at least be in the States most of the time. As much as I love going all over the world, some laws in other countries are too restrictive. You'll also get more time in your own bed." Her mouth forms a slight grin. "I assume that's something you'll be happy about."

Actually, I would be pretty happy about that. I'm in a committed relationship with my mattress. "Why hasn't anyone in management said anything to me about it?"

"Technically," her voice is a high-pitched whisper. "I'm not even supposed to know about it. I heard it through a few people. Some other attendants are being reassigned, too. They are supposed to tell us after we get back from this trip, so act surprised."

I'm not mad about it, just shocked. They normally tell us weeks in advance, so this is surprising. It'll also be nice working shorter trips. The international ones aren't horrible, but they are so freaking long. Passengers become restless, if there isn't a layover, and can get grumpy with us. As if it's our fault they decided to go to Europe with their children. That's another thing I won't miss, hours of kids asking their parents how much longer the flight will be. I have nothing against kids, but small ones can make the flight more stressful than it needs to be.

"Um, Jolene," Lana snaps her fingers in front of me. "Are you okay? You're not upset about the change, are you?"

"Not even a little bit." I swipe my lashes with a bit of mascara before throwing it in my makeup bag and putting it in my suitcase. "I have a feeling my bed and I will be able to take our relationship to the next level."

"You are so weird."

"I like uninterrupted sleep," I shrug. "The cots on the plane are just fine, but it's not exactly comfortable."

"That's an excellent point." Another announcement comes over the speakers and her eyes widen. "Shit. You need to go get dressed. Our plane is almost here and we still have to get it ready before boarding."

"And this is why I wanted to get ready at home, before I got here. I don't like being rushed."

"Well, I needed you."

"No, you didn't," I shake my head, exasperated. "You just didn't want to sit up here by yourself."

"I plead the fifth." She picks up my garment bag and shoves it in my arms. "Now go get dressed."

I don't have time to argue. I rush to the bathroom to put on my uniform. I'm going to make this the best flight I've ever had. Starting next week, I'll be back in the continental states for a while.

THREE

Bentley

I'VE LEFT the state before. We played quite a few out-of-state games when I was at Hilltown. The only difference... we're taking a plane instead of a bus. I have no idea what to expect. I've never been on one before, but I'm too stubborn to ask any of the guys for pointers.

Since we don't travel as a team, which I thought we did, we're on our own. My only saving grace has been Jordan. He offered to book my flight with his so I can travel with him. Normally, his wife, Vanessa, would go with him, but has plans with her family.

Jordan has taken me under his wing, and I think his life goal is to keep me on the straight and narrow. He says he's seen too many young players get in the game, want the finer things in life and lose it all because of wrong choices. I'm fine with that, as long as he knows I'm going to walk just outside the line. Yes, I want the finer things in life. Who doesn't? I also want to have fun. I'm not married or tied down and should be able to do what I want for the most part. Well, as long as it's legal.

My suitcase is open on my bed, and I have no idea what to pack. How do people travel like this all the time? It's something I'll have to get used to, but I'm at a loss for how it all works. We leave in the morning and if I don't get this done, I'll be standing here until then. Pulling out my phone, I google what to pack for a flight. I click on the first site that pops up, and glance over the list. There are so many things not allowed in carryon luggage. I don't want to check my baggage and look like an idiot while figuring it out. I could text Jordan and ask him what I need to do, but I don't want to come off as a complete newb. Even if that's exactly what I am. A message flashes across my screen, and I breathe a sigh of relief. Maybe this is a list of everything we need. Just what I need, help without asking for it.

Jordan: I'll be there to pick you up at 6 sharp.
Bentley: In the morning!?!
Jordan: Yes. We have to go through security and deal with our luggage.
Bentley: It can't seriously take that long.
Jordan: Have you ever flown before?
Bentley: If I say no, will you make fun of me?
Jordan: Shut up. We've all had our first time on a plane. Some just happen to take place earlier than others.
Bentley: Ok, then no. And I don't know what to pack in which bag. There are so many fucking rules.
Jordan: Here's a list of the essentials. Be ready when I get there. And wear comfortable clothes.

What the hell? The list is detailed and even has small check boxes next to each item. I never realized how organized he is. His wife is probably the one that put it together. I'm not complaining, though. It's a starting point and I need to get it done quickly so I can get some sleep tonight.

"Why are the seats so close together?" In the movies they always show them spread further apart. I mean, you at least had elbow room. I feel like a sardine in this tiny seat.

"Because, Bentley," Jordan rolls his eyes at me as he puts his seatbelt on. "We're sitting in coach."

Wait, what? Coach? We're basketball players for a professional team for crying out loud. We should be in first class. "Why aren't we in first?"

"These young ones will never learn," he mutters under his breath. "It's not so bad, and it's cheaper. One day you'll appreciate my wisdom instead of worrying about pissing away your money."

Little does he know, I'm fine with spending my money. I've never had much and is it so wrong for me to enjoy the finer things in life? "If you say so, Grandpa."

"I'm barely a decade older than you." He shakes his head and holds out a stick of gum. "I'm just trying to save you down the road. I've seen too many players spend all their money on useless things. One day you'll find a girl to settle down with and start a family. You're going to want money to support them."

"I'll keep that in mind." There's no way I'm settling down....ever. A few of the other guys on the team boarded this flight, too. Us being in coach is a clear indicator of why they got to board before us. I wish I had more world experience. Feeling like an idiot because I've never done these things is annoying. "Why did you give me gum?"

"It helps first time fliers with their ears. They may pop when we take off and land. Chewing gum helps decrease the pressure."

The pilot's voice is scratchy over the intercom. "Good morning, travelers. We're about to take off. Please look to the front as the flight attendants lead you through the safety precautions."

A few attendants walk down the small aisle and disappear behind a curtain. They must be heading to first class. A blonde passes by me, and stands at the front of the cabin. Another follows behind her and stops right in front of me. She's tall, and her long brown hair is pulled into a high ponytail. The uniform she's wearing is simple, but it hugs her body in all the right places. She turns until she's facing all of us and begins moving her arms as the speaker tells us where the masks are and how to put them on. Not exactly promising for my first time on a plane, but my eyes stay focused on her.

"Thank you," the pilot's voice comes over the speakers again. "Please fasten your seatbelts and remain seated. The attendants will be around to get your drink orders as soon as we're in the air."

The brunette woman then walks to the back of the plane and the others follow her. The plane shakes as we ascend into the air. My fingers clench the armrests and I'm chewing the gum like it's the last meal I'll ever have. I'm not cut out for this. I wonder if I can drive to the rest of our out-of-town games. Or take a train. Anything is preferable to this.

Jordan reaches up and pats my shoulder. "It's fine, Bentley. We're almost leveled out and it'll be smooth sailing from there." I hope so because this is terrifying.

Note to self, never drink as much water as I have on this flight. I have to piss, but I don't want to leave my seat. Jordan was right about the plane leveling out. It doesn't mean I want to get up and wander around the plane trying to figure out the bathroom situation. Where does it all go when people flush? All I can imagine is it falling on some unsuspecting people. My body trembles at the thought. I'm honestly shocked my mind went to such a disgusting place. Nerves will do that to anyone, though.

My legs bounce up and down, trying to keep the urge to go to the restroom at bay. I'm sure I look ridiculous doing the equivalent of the potty dance while sitting down, but I really don't want to get out of my seat. I eye the back of the plane, determining how far away the bathroom is from my seat. Son of a bitch, I'm not going to be able to hold it until we land. "Which one of those bathrooms is for dudes?" I nudge Jordan with my elbow.

He laughs and tries to cover it with his hand as if it's not obvious that he's laughing at me and not with me. "Both of them. They aren't gender specific."

"I won't like fall in or anything will I?"

The bark of laughter is too hard to cover up this time and heads turn toward us. Oh, for fuck's sake. Next time I'm researching all of this beforehand. "Never mind. I'll figure it out."

I undo my seatbelt and stand, keeping my head slightly bent so I don't hit it on the overhead compartments. These planes were not made for tall people. I'm certain this isn't a struggle my fellow teammates on this flight are dealing with since they are in first class. Booking my own flight will be added to the list of things I need to learn how to do. Jordan is not allowed to do these things for me if he's going to be a smart ass.

I'm so focused on my frustration that I'm not paying attention to what, or rather who, is in front of me until I slam right into her. The hot flight attendant from earlier. Unfortunately, she's been helping the people on the other side of the aisle and someone else helped us. The tray in her hand tips forward and my hand shoots out to steady it for her. "I'm so sorry," she says low enough that only I can hear.

"It's all good," I smile at her. "I wasn't paying attention." She's even more beautiful up close, and I want to get to know her better. Even if it's only for this plane ride. Though, she should be on other flights I take since she obviously works for the airline our team wants us to use.

"Sir," she nods her head to the aisle. "Can you let me by? I have passengers to attend to."

My cheeks flame, and I have no idea why I'm blushing. I don't have a problem talking to women, but this one stops me in my tracks. "Yeah, sure. Sorry." I turn to let her by, and the person behind me mutters "excuse you." I shift my body until I'm back in the aisle and she's walking away. "My name is Bentley, by the way."

She doesn't respond and shakes her head as she passes out drinks to the passengers. Damn. I'm on my first flight and I lose my cool. How does that even happen? Sighing, I turn back toward the bathrooms. I don't miss Jordan's snickers as I close the door behind me. That's it. I'm never traveling with that jackass again.

FOUR

Jolene

THE FLIGHT IS ALMOST over and Lana's hip bumps into mine as we dispose of the last of the cups from the passengers. "That guy over there keeps staring at you."

I don't need to look up to see who it is. I've felt his eyes on me since he ran into me on the way to the restroom. "Please," I scoff. "Do you realize how many guys check us out on each flight? It's nothing new. They all have a fantasy for what they can't have."

"Oh, you mean one of us hot, young attendants with our backs against the wall in the restroom while they tick joining the 'mile high club' off their bucket list?"

"That would be it." I can't argue and say that it's never happened. We just weren't in the air, and it wasn't a passenger. I will be happy when thoughts of Carter no longer haunt me. "It's kind of sad, really. Do they not have anything else to look forward to when they get off the plane?"

Lana shrugs and goes about cleaning up the small

refreshment area. She's quiet for a few minutes as she wipes down the counter. Just when I think she's done with the conversation, she adds. "If I'm not mistaken, he's one of the basketball players on this flight. There were a few of them in first class, but I think I've seen the guy sitting next to him on the news for something or other."

"Who cares if he plays sports? That means nothing. He's just another one of those guys with an over-inflated ego and thinks women should line up to throw themselves at him." I know one of those guys. I was with one of those guys. I can spot them a mile away thanks to a certain pilot.

"I'll remember that."

"Go ahead because *nothing* is ever going to happen with him." Dating passengers isn't necessarily against the rules, but I don't want to make a habit of hooking up with guys I'll only see once every few months. That's not a healthy relationship. Besides, I've sworn off relationships. There's no way in hell anyone can get me to change my mind. Men only add stress and take up too much brain space.

The captain's voice comes over the crackly speakers. "We are about ten minutes from our destination and we'll soon begin our descent. Passengers, please return to your seats and fasten your belts. Thank you."

A woman leaves the tiny restroom with a toddler in tow. She's pulling him toward their seats, and the kid isn't having it. He's ready to be off this plane if his pout and red face are any indication. Bentley looks around him as he fastens his seatbelt. The man sitting next to him hands him something and he quickly puts it in his mouth. It must be gum. It appears this guy, whoever he is, has never flown before. Now his flustered state in the aisle earlier makes sense. Anyone would be off kilter if they're experiencing something for the first time.

"You're checking him out," Lana whispers in my ear.

"No, I'm not."

"Yes, you are."

I'm not going to satisfy her with a reply. Just because my eyes landed on him while making sure all the passengers are doing what they are told, doesn't mean anything. Whether or not she thinks so. I take a seat on one of the foldout chairs and buckle myself in. Usually I'm the one that stays out to make sure everyone is okay while we land, but Lana is taking care of it today. She loves this job, and I don't think anyone could pull her away from it.

Me? I'm on the fence. Traveling to unfamiliar countries has been amazing, but being gone all the time is wearing me out. It's a good thing the airline picked up this partnership because that means more at home time for me.

"Thank you for flying with International Airlines today," the captain's voice isn't nearly as smooth as Carter's but it's deep and even though the speakers suck, he has a way of putting fliers at ease. "We'll begin deboarding the plane in a few minutes."

That's our cue to be ready to help any passengers that may need it and wish them safe travels as they leave the plane. I stand beside the door and wait for them to line up to get out of the small area and on to their next adventure.

The door opens and people funnel into the air bridge. Another successful flight. We have a few hours until the next one and I'm not sure what I will do for those hours. I'm sure part of it will be spent at one of the food places with Lana, listening to her go on and on about all the hot guys she's been dating. Not exactly how I want to spend my free time, but it's better than being alone with my thoughts.

The guy, Bentley, who bumped into me earlier still hasn't come through the line to depart the plane. There's no way he could have gotten lost in the cramped space. And I'm almost certain the guy sitting next to him doesn't have any issues with how flights work. Surely, I didn't miss them. I shouldn't care that they haven't come through yet, but I have a special place in my heart for the first-time fliers. It doesn't matter if they are children or older, nothing quite prepares them for how it feels to be up in the air, above everyone else, and passing through cloud after cloud.

"He's coming," Lana whisper yells in my ear. Where did she even come from? I thought she was handling the first-class people, not back here waiting for me to make a move on a guy I have no intentions of having any relationship with. Not even a quick one-night stand. It's not how I operate.

"Go do your own job," I jab her with my elbow. "I'm perfectly capable of handling a full-grown dude." Especially if that one is as good looking as this one. No. Stop that, Jolene. No men. Ever.

The man in question stops right in front of me. "I didn't catch your name earlier." He looks down at where my name tag is, and I move my hand to cover it up. Even if I were interested, I wouldn't make it that easy for him.

"That's because I didn't offer it." My lips quirk into a half-smile. I'm knowingly flirting with this man. It honestly feels great even though I know I shouldn't be doing it. "I hope you enjoyed your flight and have an amazing time in New York."

"So, would you be willing to offer your name?" There's a line of people standing behind him. Shuffling back and forth, patiently waiting to be let off the plane. I wonder if they think this is normal, or that maybe this man needs something more important besides my name.

"Come on Bentley," the tall man behind him tries to

nudge him forward, "let the woman do her job and stop stroking your ego. She's obviously not interested."

"But she smiled," he grins at me while he's talking about me as if I can't hear every word he's saying, "that has to mean something."

"It was barely a smile, and she's just being polite." He nods his head toward me. "I'm sorry about my friend here. He has a habit of not letting things go even when it's not going in his favor."

"If I didn't persist, I never would have made the team," his mouth widens, and damn it if it doesn't make him more attractive. "From what I recall none of the players liked me and were trying to talk Coach into not giving me another chance. I kept pushing and here I am. On my way to help my team get to the finals."

"See what I mean?" The friend shrugs and then places his hands on Bentley's back to push him forward.

"It's fine," I laugh. "I've known quite a few people just like him."

"I feel like I should be offended." He places his hand over his chest as if I have wounded him. He clearly doesn't know *how* to be offended. "So, are you going to give me your name, or am I going to have to hunt down your friend and ask her for the information?"

The people behind him are getting antsy. The feet shuffling has now turned into sighs and some crossing their arms over their chest, irritated that this guy is wasting their precious time. Normally, I wouldn't give into something like this. But, I know he would look for Lana, and she'd be all too happy to give him any details he wants. No, I'm going to do what needs to be done for the greater good of the rest of the passengers wanting to get off this plane. "My name is Jolene."

"Like that country song?" He tilts his head to the side and looks like a confused puppy. But I'm kind of annoyed that his first question is *that*. I've heard it a million times, and it drives me crazy each time.

"Yes," I sigh. "Just like the country song. Now, if you would," I wave my right arm toward the door. "There are other passengers waiting to leave, and you're holding up the line."

"Sorry." There's that smidge of insecurity he had when he ran into me earlier. "I'll be seeing you, Jolene. Have an exceptional day."

Because that's not creepy at all. "Yeah, you too." I swear the rest of the people on the flight want to clap their hands as he walks out of the door into the small hallway that leads to the airport. That has got to be the weirdest confrontation I've ever had. Hopefully, he's gone before I get off the plane. I do not want to deal with that mess when I have time to enjoy myself before my next flight assignment.

Why can't I be lucky just once in my life? Standing right next to my best friend is the one person I don't want to see. Carter is talking to Lana animatedly, and I don't want to interrupt. Hell, I don't know why he's even here. He rarely does domestic flights. Almost all of them are international.

"Hey, Jolene," Lana waves me over. "The Captain here was just telling me he's retiring from the business."

"What?" My voice is loud even among the chattering people around us. "You love to fly, what's making you give it up?"

"I love Kendall more than flying, and I want to start a family." He's practically glowing with happiness, and as much as it hurt when he didn't want more from me, I can't begrudge him this. "I can't very well do that if I'm always up in the clouds."

"You have a point there," Lana claps him on the back. "I wish you the best, and hopefully you'll come see us every once in a while."

"As if I would fly on any other airline," he rolls his eyes. He looks at me and asks, "How have you been, Jolene?"

That's not what I was expecting to come out of his mouth. "Huh?" I take a minute to gather my composure. "Fine. We were switched to more domestic flights since IA partnered with this basketball team. I get to see my bed more." I cringe. What the actual hell? That makes me sound desperate, and that's not how I want to sound.

A figure crosses my peripheral and it's none other than Bentley. His eyes catch mine and I wave him over. "Speaking of, this is one of the players from the team. Bentley, this is Carter."

Carter furrows his brow, confused as to why I'm introducing him to this guy he'll never see again. "It's, um, nice to meet you."

"You too," Bentley doesn't miss a beat. He throws his arm around my shoulder and pulls me closer to him. I squeak at the close contact and Lana is doing everything in her power not to burst out in laughter. "How do you know my sweet Jolene?"

Oh. My. God. Please, someone, wake me up from this nightmare. I didn't mean to imply that we were dating. Carter's smile returns, "We used to work together. I'm, as of this weekend, a retired captain."

"Wow," Bentley's eyes widen. "You're so young."

"Thanks...I think." He holds his hand up and waves to

us. "It's time for me to get out of here. Kendall's waiting for me in the bar."

"Of course, she is," I mutter under my breath.

Lana can no longer hold the laughter in and she bends over in a fit of giggles. "That was hysterical."

I slide out from under Bentley's arm and put as much distance as I can between us. "Why did you tell him I was yours? I barely met you twenty minutes ago."

"You looked like you needed a little help." He takes a step closer to me and I take a step back toward Lana. "Besides, maybe since I covered for you, with what seems to be an ex-boyfriend, you'll go out on a date with me."

"That's not happening." The words are out of my mouth as soon as he half-ass makes the suggestion. "I don't date guys I barely know. Besides, you don't even live here. How would that work out?"

"Technically, you don't live here, either," Lana points out.

"Shut up, Lana. That's beside the point." I turn toward the man that literally helped me out of an awkward situation and point my finger at him. "I don't have time to date anyone. In case you haven't noticed, I'm busy flying around and doing my job."

"Maybe a fake date, at least. In the hotel bar to really sell it to the dude who just left."

This guy is relentless. I knew I shouldn't have told him my name. "I don't need to sell it to him. He's perfectly happy in his relationship. I was originally going to introduce you as one of the players we're now flying around. *You* are the one who implied you were my boyfriend."

"I know when to back down." He bows slightly, but the smile never leaves his face. "Until next time."

What does he mean by next time? Lana can't control herself any longer. "You really stepped in it that time."

"What do you mean?"

Wiping a tear, did she have to laugh that hard, from her eye she shakes her head. "I'm looking forward to how this will play out."

Nope. There's nothing to play out. The area around my heart is man free. There's no way I'm opening myself up to that hurt again.

FIVE

Bentley

Jordan sighs as we walk out of the airport and shakes his head. "Go ahead and tell me whatever is on your mind. I know you're dying to." The vibe off of him is weird. It's almost something I think most disappointed dads would look like when they are upset with their kid. Never knowing my dad, I didn't have that look, even though my mom shot it at me often enough.

"Learn when to shut up and move on. You'll be lucky if that woman doesn't go to her bosses and claim harassment."

That thought never crossed my mind, and it isn't something I've really had to deal with. It's usually me that has to keep my distance from women when they push for dates. I've rarely turned any of them down, but there are a few that just wouldn't stop. Is that what I've turned into? The person who won't stop. No, that can't be it. She smiled when she teased me about her name. And...she's the one who pulled me into whatever conversation she was having. "Naw, man. She was having fun, too."

"Maybe, but you also didn't give her much of a choice." He pulls the door open on the cab and ushers me to go in first. "Just keep that in mind next time."

I make a face and slide into the seat. He's not my father, and not even close to being old enough for that. But why do I feel like a scolded child being sent to time out? I shake the thought away and turn my focus to our upcoming game. We have a shoot around in a few hours and my mental headspace needs to be on that. Not the hot girl I met on a plane.

She keeps slipping into my thoughts as we make our way past tall buildings at a snail's speed. Austin's traffic is horrible, but this is a completely new level of people. The streets are jammed with cars, and the sidewalks are packed with people. Who knew New York was so much busier than our own city? Most people know that saying "everything's bigger in Texas," but this puts us to shame. The buildings soar high into the sky and lights are flashing everywhere. A part of me wonders if this is the sort of city Jolene lives in. So much for focusing on basketball. That's obviously going to be a lost cause.

Finally, after what feels like forever, the cab comes to a stop in front of what I assume is our hotel. Jordan pays him and we get out of the car. Jordan goes around to pull our bags out of the trunk and we walk toward the building. "I really hope we have rooms on one of the lower floors. I don't know if I'd be able to stay in one of the upper rooms."

"It's not so bad," Jordan chuckles. "You can't even tell you're up that high as long as you don't look out the window."

"Any chance there's an interior room where I won't be tempted?" I don't like heights. I've never been a fan of rollercoasters and anything like that. My sister had to drag me onto the slides at the water park we went to as kids, and I screamed the entire way.

"You'll be fine. Don't even stress." He stops in front of the hotel doors and looks back at me. "If you get too scared, I can always come tuck you in."

"Shut up, asshole." He doesn't reply and continues inside, laughing loud enough that everyone turns their head toward him. How in the hell did I get stuck with him? Oh yeah, he was the only person on the team that would talk to me when I was first signed on.

The wheel of my suitcase sticks and I yank it behind me as I enter the lobby. I'm too busy making sure that it's not falling apart as I walk that I don't notice anyone is in front of me until I run right into them. "Sorry," I say before looking up.

"Hey, you're that guy from the plane."

What the hell? I'm not even that popular. At least, I don't think I am...yet. I'm barely getting play time, and there's no way someone from a different state would know who I am. I pause messing with my suitcase and look up. "You're Jolene's friend, right?"

"Yeah, Lana." She holds her hand out, "We didn't get to properly meet while at the airport."

"Bentley," I place my hand in hers and shake. "The airline puts you up in some swanky hotels." This place has to be expensive. I know if I wasn't on the team, there's no way I'd be able to afford to even walk into a place like this.

"I'm meeting a friend."

"Is Jolene with you?" I turn my head to the left and right, hoping to glimpse the woman who wants nothing to do with me.

"No, she's at the airport hotel." She bounces on her toes,

waiting for me to say something else. When I don't, she grins. "So, that entire thing didn't go as you planned, did it?"

"Honestly, I'm surprised she pulled me to y'all. What's the story with her and that dude?"

"It's not my place to say anything, but a good way to impress her is maybe don't be so...abrasive."

Jordan said the same thing. Maybe I am overbearing when it comes to something, or in this case someone, I want. "I don't know if I'll ever see her again. There's no guarantee she'll be working anymore on the flights I'm on."

"Lucky for you, I can help with that." She pulls out her phone and opens up her contacts. "Give me your number." Oh no. I really hope she's not trying to pull one over on me and blow up my phone to date her. She must see my hesitancy because she adds, "If you want my help with Jolene, I'll need your number to pass along information."

She has a point. She hasn't shown the slightest hint that she's interested in me. I breathe out a sigh of relief and rattle off my number. "Why are you willing to help me?"

My phone dings in my pocket and Lana slides her phone back into her pocket. "Because she's had a rough go of it lately, and I'll do anything to put a smile on her face. Even if it's only to have some fun with you." Should I be offended she's insinuating I'm only around for a good time? She's not wrong, but I don't like how easily she's pegged me. "Just don't hurt her if you can help it."

"That's never my goal." Taking a step closer to her, I nod my head. "Thank you for your help. I'm not even sure why I like her. It's probably because she won't give me the time of day." That makes her a challenge whether she knows it or not. "I better catch up with my friend. I have no idea what I'm doing. It's my first out-of-town game."

"Good luck," she waves at me. "I know nothing about sports, but I hope you win."

"Thanks." I watch her walk away, toward one of my teammates. That's odd. Shrugging my shoulders, I search for Jordan. He's in line at the front desk, and I make my way toward him. As grateful as I am for Lana's help, that has to be the weirdest conversation I've ever had. She'll either come through with the help, or she'll forget I exist. Only time will tell.

~

"Rookie," the coach calls. I'm toward the end of the long row of chairs, and unsure if I heard him correctly. There isn't anyone else he could be talking to. I'm the only rookie on the team. "Get over here."

One of my teammates slaps my arm. "You better go. He wants to put you on the court."

Standing up, I pull my off my warmup pants, almost tripping over the last snap that won't undo. Throwing the pants on the chair I was sitting in; I turn toward the coach and jog over. "Yeah, Coach."

"I need you to go in," he puts a hand on my shoulder. "If you want to move up to a starting position, you need to show me you want it. Jump in for Hobbs, and we'll see how you do."

"You got it, Coach." I don't wait to see if he has anything else to say. Everything he said after 'I need you to go in' went in one ear and out the other. I check in with the score table and wait for the refs to wave me in.

Hobbs isn't happy that he's being taken out of the game to be replaced with the new guy, but I don't really care. This is my chance to shine. He also had to have known that his shitty playing would get him pulled from the game. Jordan is smiling as I join the rest of the players on the court. I roll my eyes and take my position.

Jordan throws the ball in from the side and I run a screen to set up the play, then sprint to baseline outside the three-point line. Nobody is guarding me, and I wait for Ross to pass me the ball for the shot, but he passes it to someone else. He saw me. I know he did. He looked right at me and chose to give the ball to someone who is heavily guarded. How am I supposed to prove myself if the rest of my team won't give me the chance?

The other team steals the ball and I haul ass to the other side of the court, hoping to get there before they score. Doing everything I can to stay in the game. Coach wants to see what I'm capable of...I'm about to make sure he sees me as an asset. Bypassing the guy with the ball, I head straight to the key. That's my sweet spot. I may not be as tall as some of these guys, but I'm not short either. All I need is for them to pass the ball and I'll block whoever thinks they're going to one up me. The point guard passes it to a player behind me and I'm quick to turn around. He sees me and tries for a jump shot. My feet leave the ground and my hands reach out to the empty air above me. For a split second I think I jumped too early, but the ball connects with my hand and I knock it out of bounds.

As much as I try to keep from looking toward the bench, I can't help it. His approval means a lot since he's the one who fought for me to be signed to the team. The coach is clapping and rolling his hand in front of him, signaling "let's go". We set up our defense as the opposing team throws the ball in. Jordan steals it and heads back to our side of the court. I'm the first one down the court. These guys may have experience, but I have speed. Training any free moment I had at Hilltown is paying off right now.

Jordan long passes the ball to me. I dribble the ball. Once. Twice. Three times. The ball is in my hands and I take three long strides before jumping. My arms are up and I bring the ball down. My fingers grip the rim, and I hang for a second before letting go, landing on my toes. The crowd boos and I forget for a second that we aren't on our home court.

Five entire minutes have passed since the first dunk of my NBA career and I'm already back on the bench. Hobbs went back in and I was forced to warm the seat I vacated not too long ago. I'm trying not to get mad about it, but I was doing good. There's no reason I should have been pulled out of the game. Unless…he was trying to teach Hobbs a lesson and show him he's replaceable. Coaches have done that since I was in high school, and I hated it then. Who knew they did it at this level, too?

The buzzer at the end of the game sounds throughout the stadium. Fans of the other team began leaving about three minutes ago when they realized they weren't going to win. My feet haven't touched the court since Coach pulled me out, but I've been paying attention. Watching what the other players do and trying to figure out what I can improve on so I can get more play time.

The team heads toward the locker room and the coach gives us a speech about how well we played, and I ignore most of it. I failed at picking up a date with the woman on the airplane, and at being able to stay in the game. Even though the team won, I can't help but feel defeated by the entire day. Once the coach walks out, my teammates and I change clothes. I want nothing more than to go to the hotel room, watch the highlights from the game, and fall asleep.

First, I need to call Mom and Gabby. I want to know if they saw me, and what they thought. They love me more than anything, but they aren't afraid to tell me where I need to brush up my skill.

To my shock, there's a message on my phone. I slide my finger across the screen to open it, ninety percent sure it's a text from Derrick, my college roommate. We've done a decent job of staying in touch since I graduated. He wouldn't have made the team if I was drilling him hard before tryouts.

The text isn't from him, though, and I don't recognize the number.

Unknown: Hey, it's Lana. I'm sending a pic of Jolene's flight schedule for the next couple of weeks. Don't do anything to screw it up.

And just like that. My whole day has turned around.

SIX

Jolene

"Good morning, Jolene." Bentley nods his head at me before walking down the aisle and taking a seat next to the window. He doesn't wait for a response from me. I wonder what that is all about. I knew being on the same flight as him would be inevitable. His team is flying exclusively with our airline. I just didn't think it would be so soon.

I eye him warily before turning to the rest of the passengers and welcoming them aboard the plane. This job is easy for the most part, repetitive, but easy. I skipped college and ran off to travel the world the cheapest way I knew how, but I'm getting bored with the same thing every single day. Maybe it's because I'm getting older. I want to settle down somewhere, I just don't know where to start. I've lived in my apartment for over three years and I can't name any of my neighbors. That's how rarely I'm home. How am I supposed to figure out my life when my only support system is also a flight attendant who craves adventure?

"You look like you're thinking too hard." Lana bumps

me from behind. "You know there aren't any more passengers coming on board, right?"

The hall in front of me is empty. "Sorry, it's a habit waiting for those last few stragglers rushing toward the gate."

"You thinking about the hunky basketball player sitting right over there?" She points to the man in question.

"Not really. Just life in general."

"That sounds like way less fun. You should be fantasizing about all the ways you can get him in bed." She laughs and thrusts her hips like a hormonal teen.

"Last time I did that, the man dropped me like I was nothing." I shake my head and sigh. "I'll do anything to keep from going down that road again." He made a fool out of me. No, I made a fool out of myself. I knew what kind of man Carter was and I willingly threw myself at him. All hoping to make him settle down with me. I won't make that mistake again. Bentley has *player* written all over him, and not in a way that describes his profession. My heart will stay perfectly caged within my chest, thank you very much.

Lana sighs and places a hand on my arm. "You can't let one bad experience ruin you for life. No man is worth that. You learn and move on. That's all you can do."

"This is me learning. All that happens when I chase down a man's attention is heartbreak and tears. I don't want that."

"Then how about you go into new relationships as something fun. No strings. Just out for a good time. If you end up in the sack, great. If you end up as something more, even better. But just go out and do something that doesn't involve drinking wine at a bar with only me."

"But I enjoy drinking with you," I pout. It's not a lie. She's really the only friend I have. It's hard to make new friends when you're constantly working. She has the ability to fit in wherever we are and I just can't do that.

"I refuse to be your only drinking date." She points toward the front of the cabin as the pilot's voice comes over the intercom. "We need to go do our thing. We'll continue this discussion later."

"No, we won't. You're working first class again."

She shrugs her shoulders. "It's nice up there. I'll see you when we get off this plane." She rushes down the aisle and disappears behind the curtain that separates first class from coach. I used to work that area, but I couldn't get over the arrogant asshole men that I encountered way too often. The ones who thought they had a right to anything, and everything, they wanted.

I make my way down my aisle and stop in the middle. I don't like being the one at the front or back; they are usually the ones that give the whole spiel while making the motions. I'm not about that life right now. The least visible I am...the better. And being in this spot gives me a chance to watch Bentley when he's not aware.

The guy that was with him last time isn't with him today and the poor guy looks like he's uncomfortable. There's a little girl sitting next to him and she's squeezing a stuffed animal close to her chest. He leans down until he's almost face to face with her. I'm close enough that I can hear the conversation.

"Is this your first time flying?" His voice is gentle. The little girl nods her head and hugs her bear tighter. "It'll be okay. This is only my third time, and I'm still nervous. We'll get through this flight together."

The little girl looks up at him, eyes wide, and clearly doesn't believe anything he's saying. Bentley reaches into his backpack and pulls out a package of gum. He looks to the girl's mom and asks, "Is it okay if I give her this."

She smiles and looks down at her daughter. "Of course. My husband is flying into his hometown today from deployment. We wanted to surprise him. I didn't realize how scared she would be."

"It's okay. My first flight was a few weeks ago, and if it hadn't been for my friend, I'm sure I would have curled up into a ball."

"I'm glad you're here to help ease her fears. I flew all the time before I had her, and she doesn't always believe what I say."

Bentley laughs. "I had a similar conversation with my friend." He holds out the pack of gum and offers it to the little girl. "Here you go. If you chew it, your ears won't pop when we lift off."

"Thank you," she squeaks out as she takes a piece and shoves it into her mouth.

We're done with our safety precautions, and the pilot announces for everyone to prepare for takeoff. I won't lie, what he did for that girl melted my heart just the tiniest bit. I'm sure he doesn't have any kids. At least, nothing I googled showed that he did. Doing that was probably a terrible idea, but I needed to know more about him. If anything, to prove that my first impression of him was correct. Every image I found of him since he joined the team is with a different girl. That's not exactly compelling evidence for me to want to consider a date with him. He's obviously not like that all the time if his interaction with the little girl is any sign.

The plane starts down the runway and I see Bentley's body tense and his hands grip the armrest. The child next to him grabs hold of her mom's hand and squeezes it tight. She looks over at Bentley before setting her bear next to her and places her hand on his arm. My heart is now mush. I quickly make my way to the back of the plane and take my seat until we are in the air. Seeing a softer side to him should not change the way I see him, but I'd be lying if I said it didn't. At least a little bit.

We've finally landed, and people are getting off the plane. Those who are seasoned at this are already off and doing whatever it is they came here to do. Bentley is still sitting with the woman and her daughter. I'm sure she's waiting until there are fewer people since she has to make sure her little one has all of her stuff.

Bentley and the girl are laughing, and a bar from the cage around my heart disappears. Oh no, that shit needs to go right back where it was. I'm not letting this guy get under my skin. Now that most of the passengers are gone, Bentley and his seatmates can get into the aisle. While the mom is getting her daughter situated, Bentley reaches above them to the bins, and pulls out his suitcase as well as the suitcase for the mom and child.

Another wall is destroyed. He pulls out his phone and taps something on it. Before showing it to the girl. The mom and child are now heading toward the exit, and the girl is carrying one of our napkins with ink scrawled across it. He must have autographed it for her.

They near me and they are both beaming. "I hope y'all had a great flight, and hope you have fun while you're in Chicago."

"Thank you. I had no idea athletes flew on regular planes. It looks like my family and I have plans tonight, now."

"What do you mean?" It's weird that they wouldn't have plans before they got here. Most people have an entire itinerary set out before they leave home.

"Bentley plays for the visiting team, and he set tickets up for us and my husband, who just got back from deployment, to go to the game tonight." Her smile is gigantic, and I can tell that it means a lot to her.

"That's great. I hope all three of you have a fantastic time at the game tonight."

"Thank you."

My eyes fall on the man of the hour and he's now helping an older woman get her luggage from the carry-on bin. This is such a different side of him than I saw when we first met last week. Maybe he's not as arrogant as he appears. When the woman reaches for her suitcase, he waves her off and tells her to go ahead of him.

They walk down the aisle, slowly, and finally make it to me. "I hope you both had a great flight."

"Thank you, Dear. This is one of my favorite airlines to fly with." The lady gives me a curt nod and takes a few steps into the hallway.

"That's good to hear."

Bentley rushes toward her, and asks, "Can you give me just a second I'll bring your luggage out to you at the gate." She glances at him and then me before grinning and shuffling along down the hall.

"When did you become such a hero?" I roll my eyes as he lopes back toward me.

He stops in his tracks and puts his hands to his heart. "You wound me."

"Please," I laugh. "Don't act like you weren't doing that for my benefit." It's the only reason I can come up with.

What other person is that helpful without getting anything in return?

"My mom would beat me into next week if I saw someone struggling and didn't offer to help. I'm not a total asshole." He leans against the doorway and looks straight into my eyes. "The fact that you saw it is just a bonus. Maybe you'll go on a date with me."

"Bentley," I sigh and lift my hand to my temple. "I already told you, I don't date." How many ways do I have to spell it out for him? Dating leads to heartbreak. I don't care what Lana says.

"You know, you can't let whatever asshole hurt you win. By shutting yourself off, that's all you're doing. Believe me, I have experience with it." A flash of sadness crosses his eyes, and I want to know who hurt him so badly.

Damn it, Jolene. No, you don't. His life is none of your concern, even if he has a point. "Look, I have to get this plane cleaned up before the next flight."

"Point taken," he mutters under his breath. "Do you have a pen and piece of paper?"

I'm not sure where he's going with this, but I pull both out of my pocket and hand them to him. If he doesn't leave soon, the next flight will be delayed, and we'll get bitched at. He scribbles something down and hands both back to me. "What's this?"

"My number," he deadpans. I'm sure he had some other smartass remark to add to it, but decided not to say it. "I'll be here for the next two days. If you change your mind about the date while I'm here, or any other time, you know how to reach me. The ball is in your court now." He doesn't say anything else. He grabs the woman's suitcase, and his, and walks down the hall without a care in the world.

A part of me wants to crumple the paper up and toss it

in the trash. I almost do, but Lana shows up out of nowhere and stops me. "You're going to want to keep that."

"Why?" Apparently, my best friend hasn't gotten the no dating memo either. Otherwise, she wouldn't be hounding me so hard about this.

"Because you need to date. You need to get over being cast aside. Do it on your terms." She stares me down, waiting for an argument, but I will let her say her piece. "You hold all the cards and can take a date with him as far as you want. Something out of the ordinary will be good for you, even if you can't see that now."

"When did you turn into such a wise woman about relationships?"

She laughs as she picks up trash from the seats. "Nobody said anything about a relationship. I'm the queen of casual dating. You just have to figure out what exactly you're looking for?"

That's the problem. I have no idea what I want out of life. I only know that constantly being on the move is no longer it.

SEVEN

Bentley

ANOTHER WIN for the Austin Rattlers name. I actually had
a decent amount of playing time during the game. Much
better than the last out-of-town game where I was in a
whole two minutes before Coach had pulled me. The only
thing that could brighten my day is a text from Jolene. Not
that I would know it was her since she didn't offer her
number.

Jordan walks out of the stadium with me. We go
through the back entrance to keep away from cameras. Even
though we won, he's not a big fan of the spotlight and will
always find ways to dip out of interviews if he can help it.
"When are you and the Mrs. heading back home?"

"Tomorrow night. She wants to do some sightseeing
before we leave." He shakes his head and smiles. "I don't
know what's left for her to see. This isn't the first time she's
been here." He looks over his shoulder at me, "What time
are you leaving?"

"Not until Sunday afternoon."

"You're not still chasing that girl, are you?" The car he ordered for us is sitting at the curb, and we climb in. "How many times does she have to tell you she's not interested?"

"Until I actually believe it." I pull my phone out of my pocket, hoping to see a message from her. "You should have seen the way she kept watching me on the flight today. Tell me that doesn't mean something."

"She could be freaked out. Did you tell her how you got her flight schedule?"

"Of course not. I'm not an idiot." Seriously, this isn't my first time trying to get a girl's attention. Well, not since college, but that was doomed before it even started. "If Lana wants to tell her, she will."

"Well, if you don't hear from your flight attendant, you're free to join me and Vanessa tomorrow."

"I don't want to be the third wheel." These two are so in love it's sickening. I've never felt that way about anyone. The only people who hold my heart are my mom and sister, and I intend to keep it that way.

"You won't be. If anything, you'll be someone I can talk to while she goes into the fifteen million small shops that catch her eye." He grins at me, "Then you can also help me carry her crap everywhere."

"So, what you're saying is, you need me to be a pack mule."

"You won't be the only one. She'll have my arms full, too."

We arrive at the hotel and step out of the car. Even if I'm carrying his wife's stuff, it'll be better than sitting at the hotel waiting for a phone call, or text, that's probably never going to come. "Sure, I'll join you."

"Thank God," Jordan sighs in relief. "You have no idea how much I was dreading going by myself."

"Are you sure Vanessa won't get mad I'm tagging along?"

"I'm sure. For some reason she actually likes you," He gives me a once over, "I can't see why. You're arrogant as hell."

"When you're good, you're good. Can't fight nature."

"And that will be your downfall. The wrong girl will come sniffing around, and you'll chase that whim until you're screwed."

He doesn't seem to think highly of me sometimes, and the criticism stings. He's the only one on the team that's accepted me and knowing that he thinks so little of me, makes me wonder if he does truly like for me to be around. "That's why I don't jump into serious relationships."

"And what is this flight attendant? I've seen women throw themselves at you for the past week, and you haven't batted an eye at them." He opens the door to the hotel and walks toward the elevator. It's late and there aren't many people in the lobby. "That's not like you. The Bentley I know is very much action first and asks questions later. Do you think holding out on who you are will make her want to be with you? She clearly already has an opinion of you, and nothing you do is going to change that."

"I'm not trying to jump into anything serious with her. She's an objective. Never in my life has anyone ever turned me down, especially now that I'm semi-famous."

"That, my friend, is dangerous territory."

"Nobody said it wasn't, but I can't get her out of my head. Maybe it's because she won't give me the time of day."

"Good luck, man." He pats me on the arm and heads to the elevator. "I'll see you bright and early. If you want, you can get Vanessa's opinion on Jolene. I'm sure she'll have a lot to say."

"No, thanks. I have a feeling she'll chew my ass out more than you have."

Laughing, he presses the button to slide the doors open. "You'd be correct. See you tomorrow." He walks in the elevator and the doors close behind him.

There's no way I'll be able to sleep anytime soon, even though I'm usually exhausted after playing. There's light music coming from the hotel bar, and a drink sounds perfect right now. Heading toward the bar, I pass a few couples going to their rooms, and as much as I don't do relationships, it'd be nice to have someone to celebrate my minor accomplishments with. I pull out one of the bar stools and wave the bartender over, "Can I get a Crown & Coke?"

"Sure thing." He rounds the bar and works on my order. My eyes find the television in the corner of the room playing highlights from the game tonight. It's surreal seeing myself on a sports news broadcast. I'm no stranger to watching myself on video. Hell, it's how I've improved my game over the years. Seeing exactly where you messed up, and what you need to fix, is how you end up in the Pros. He slides a glass in front of me. "Here you go, sir."

"Thanks." I stare into the glass, wondering how I ended up drinking alone in a hotel bar, before I take a long drink. Oh, that's right, because I'm trying to get a girl that has no interest in me to go on a date.

Damn, Jordan just had to make me doubt my plan for Jolene. Being a straight up asshole isn't my goal. I genuinely want to go out with her. She's not afraid to speak her mind and has zero issues going toe-to-toe with me. It's refreshing. The only other woman who has ever done that is Gabby, and she doesn't count because she's my sister.

He's right, though. I should nip this thing in the bud and not pressure this woman to go out with me. At some point it has to be creepy, right? Lana seemed to think it was a good idea, though. Surely her best friend would know whether I'm pushing my limits. Most women try to protect their friends from someone they think is a jerk, not push them together.

The sad thing is...I'm not a hundred percent sure how we would even date if it ever went past the first one. Jordan is right. This is stupid, and I should let it go. There are plenty of women jumping at the chance to go out with me. I shouldn't be so focused on this one woman who can't even stand me.

The bartender comes back around to me, and nods toward the now empty glass. "Want another one?"

I have to meet Jordan in the morning, and it's probably not a good idea, but who cares? It's not like I absolutely have to go. "Sure, thanks."

The bartender returns a few moments later with my drink. "Here you go." He glances at the TV and then back at me. "You played one hell of a game tonight, even if you're not who I was rooting for."

"Thank you?" It comes out more like a question. It's the weirdest compliment I think I've ever received, especially coming from a fan of the opposing team.

"You have a pretty solid game considering you're a rookie." He leans an elbow on the bar, and glances around to make sure nobody else needs anything. "How are you so good at such a young age?"

I laugh. As odd as this conversation is, it's nice talking about the sport I love with someone not on my team, or in my family, for that matter. "A lot of practice. I've played since I was a kid and trained every chance I could when I was in college. Even during off season."

"It shows." He nods his head toward the TV, "I'm surprised they don't play you more."

"You aren't the only one," I mutter under my breath, hoping he doesn't hear me.

A man in a suit waves his hand across the bar to signal he wants a drink, and I feel underdressed. The hotel is fancy. I'm not sure I'll ever get used to staying in places like this. One day, maybe, but today is not that day. My joggers and t-shirt definitely have no business in this setting when other patrons are dressed to the nines.

The bartender raps his knuckles against the bar top. "If you need anything, wave me down." And just like that, our court talk is over. I've had a lot of crazy conversations, but that one...it popped out of nowhere and ended just as abruptly.

Sipping on my drink, the events of the day flash through my mind. The only one that stands out is Jolene's hand wrapped around the paper with my phone number. Either she'll call, or she won't. If she doesn't, that'll be my sign that I need to give up my farce. I already booked my flights for the next few weeks, and they all happen to have her working them. If it doesn't work out in my favor, I'll play it off as wanting to make sure I get to my games early. It's not a total lie. I like arriving for the games well in advance. It gives me a chance to get in the right mental space and prepare myself for success. Or at least give me more of the coach's approval. If there's one person I've always looked up to, it's whoever is coaching the team I'm on. It could be because they are like a father-figure to me since I didn't have one growing up. Who knows? But their thoughts of me are part of what fuels me.

I pull my wallet out of my pocket and throw some bills on the bar. This is turning into a woe is me pity party, and it's something that should not be done in public. A yawn escapes my lips, and that's the next signal that I need to go up to my room.

Halfway across the lobby, my phone dings and my heart skips. It's either Jolene or Jordan. I'm hoping for the former, but it's most likely the latter. Sliding the phone out of my pocket, I check the screen. Unknown number. Hmm, it's definitely not Jordan. I open up the screen and grin.

Unknown: I guess I'll go out on a date with you.
Bentley: Don't make it sound like I twisted your arm.

I take a moment to save the phone number to my phone. Now I have a way to get a hold of her directly.

Jolene: You kind of did. But I'm free until around lunch on Sunday.
Bentley: Lunch tomorrow?
Jolene: Sure.
Bentley: Just tell me where and I'll be there.
Jolene: Let me see what's in this town and I'll let you know in the morning.
Bentley: Sounds good. Goodnight Jolene.

She doesn't respond, but I know she's interested now, and that's all that matters. So much for Jordan's words of wisdom on the ride over from the stadium. He and Vanessa are practically high school sweethearts. How would he know what works in the dating world?

The text from Jolene is all I needed to give me a boost of energy. I don't know if I'll go to bed for different reasons now. I know nothing about Chicago and foresee the rest of the night spent on google searching for things to do. But first, I need to text Jordan.

Bentley: Slight change of plans for tomorrow. I can hang out until lunch. Then I have a date.
Jordan: Did you pick up a girl from the bar?
Bentley: Nope. SHE texted me.
Jordan: Cool. Can I go back to sleep now?
Bentley: Sure, old man.

The middle finger emoji is all that shows up when he texts me back. I'm doing this skip walk thing as I head toward the elevators. There's nothing in the world that can wipe the smile off my face. Tomorrow will be epic.

EIGHT

Jolene

I can't believe I'm doing this. What sane woman, who has sworn off men, agrees to a date with a guy they don't even know if they actually like? Oh, that's right...me. What does one even wear to a lunch date? It's been so long since I've had to get dressed for an actual date. With Carter, things were different. We shed out of our uniforms and jumped straight into bed. No outings or formal dates. That should have been my first clue he wasn't as serious about me as I was about him.

I wish him nothing but the best, I just don't know that I'll ever stop comparing everything, and everyone, to him. Or how long it'll take me to truly see the new him. The one that is in a relationship full of love and adoration. It looks good on him. I only have to remember that Bentley isn't him. This date is just that...a date. There will be no wondering about our future, or clinging onto him because he's showing me attention. I can do this. I can have fun without becoming dependent. I have to do it this way for my sanity.

"You aren't wearing that, are you?" Lana walks into the room we're sharing at the airport hotel.

"What's wrong with it?" It's a three-quarter sleeve floral dress that has a small bit of give to it. It doesn't cling to my body or make my body look unflattering.

She laughs and quickly covers her mouth as the door shuts behind her. "I'm sorry. That was bitchy." She waves her hands up and down my body. "Nothing about that dress screams sex appeal."

"That's kind of the point," I argue. "I'm not trying to land in his bed and be another notch on his bedpost."

"It also defeats the purpose of having fun. I know damn well you aren't frumpy and that's what this monstrosity portrays." She crosses the room to her suitcase and flings the top open. "If you don't have any acceptable clothes, we'll either have to go on a quick shopping trip, or you'll have to wear something of mine."

"There's no way your clothes will fit me. I'm taller than you and my boobs are bigger. Anything you give me will make me look like I'm trying to dress like a teenager."

"Looks like we're going shopping then." A sinister smile crosses her face and I don't like whatever she has planned.

My eyes lock on the alarm clock sitting between our beds, and I shake my head. "There isn't time." Is my dress really that bad? I don't think he'd have an issue with it. My thoughts flash back to the gossip sites I saw him on. In almost every single one of them the women he was with were in skin tight dresses and dressed to the nines. Surely, he isn't expecting that from me. "Besides it's only a lunch date. It's not like we're going out for a night on the town."

"That you know of," she winks at me.

"What do you mean?" My words are rushed and now I'm freaking out.

"I mean," she grins, "if you end up having fun on your lunch date, who says it has to stop there? It could continue on throughout the rest of the day. You might want to be prepared for that."

Not. Going. To. Happen. He's a player and I would be an idiot to think our date will go further than that. I'm using this as an excuse to fulfill my curiosity. That's all it is. Once I see that he's exactly the way I have him pegged, despite calming little girls and helping old ladies with their luggage, I'll be free to dislike him once and for all. Especially if my reasons are valid. "Remember how you told me to take it one step at a time and do what feels right for me?" Her eyebrows furrow, not sure where I'm going with this conversation, and she nods. "This is me doing just that. I will not change myself to go on a date with him. He either likes me, or he doesn't. Forcing myself to fit into what I think he might like is going against what I'm comfortable with."

"But..." She begins, but I hold my hand up to stop her.

"No 'buts'. I'm not like you. I don't do well in any situation. If I happen to enjoy his company, then we'll see where it goes. But I'm not going to plan for anything more than meeting him to eat lunch."

"I guess." She crosses her arms over her chest and pouts. "But you have to fill me in on everything when you get back to the room. I want every juicy detail."

"I promise." It's not like I have anyone else to tell. I haven't talked to my parents in ages, and I'm not close to my siblings either. As far as I'm concerned, Lana is my best friend and family. "Have your phone handy in case I need a quick escape."

She pulls it out of her pocket and waves it in the air. "Of

course, just like the old times before you let one man zap the fun out of you."

That was a low blow, and her eyes widen in shock once she realizes what she said. "I have to go or I'll be late." I point at the phone in her hand, "And don't forget to answer that if I text or call."

"Got it. Now, go have fun. Live a little and let your hair down."

I hate that saying. Like having it up somehow makes you uptight all of a sudden. Oh well, I don't have time to think about the semantics of a stupid saying. I need to get this show on the road. The sooner I'm done with this date, the sooner I can come back to the room and binge watch Netflix.

The pizza parlor is packed, and I'm regretting my choice for lunch. I tried to pick somewhere close to downtown. It's easy access for both of us and I can hightail it back to my hotel if I need to. I'm unsure of where exactly I'm supposed to meet him. It's something I forgot to mention in our text messages.

Jolene: I'm walking in. Are you here?
Bentley: Yes, I have a table in the back. There are a ton of people in here. Want me to walk up front to get you?
Jolene: I'm capable of walking in there on my own.
Bentley: Too late.

I look up and Bentley's smiling face is right in front of me, separated only by the glass door. "Hi," he yells through it and waves.

Angling my head toward the ground to keep him from seeing the grin I'm wearing; I shake my head. This man is full of surprises, and I'm not sure if that is a good or bad thing. Bad. Definitely a bad thing. If he worms his way into my heart, I'm not sure I can stop myself from catching feelings. Now that I've composed myself, I lift my head and open the door. "Hi."

People are milling about, but as we walk in, they stare at us. I lean over and whisper in his ear, "Why are they looking at us?"

He shrugs his shoulders as if he has no idea. "Maybe they aren't used to seeing such a pretty face." He smiles at me as he says that, except I know a bull crap line when I hear one.

It's part of the job as a flight attendant. So many men try to smooth talk their way into free alcohol or try to get in our pants. I've heard everything, and his statement does nothing but put me on high alert. "You should probably be a little more original."

"I am as original as it gets. I've never tried being something that I'm not." His voice is gruff with a bit of sadness mixed in.

I didn't mean to offend him, but come on who says that to a woman they've literally just met? "If you say so." He continues leading me through the throng of people until we are at a table in the back corner, just like he said.

"Which side do you want to sit on?"

"It doesn't matter to me. One side is no better than the other." He walks around the table and pulls out the chair closest to the wall, waiting until I sit down before going back around and sitting with his back to the rest of the restaurant. "It's strange that you picked that seat."

He picks up the menu and begins scanning it. "Why do you say that?"

I pick up another menu from the table and lift it until it covers most of my face. It's not because I'm nervous, well, not completely. I just don't want to give away too many facial expressions. Shrugging my shoulders, I look over the menu. "I don't know, most of the men in my family, or even men I see at restaurants, rarely like to sit with their backs facing the door."

He smirks but doesn't lift his eyes from the laminated paper in his hands. "Normally, that would be true. But, since I began playing pro, it's a lot easier for me to get through a meal without being recognized if I'm not facing the entire restaurant."

Huh, I guess I never thought about it like that before. Then again, I've never gone out on a date with anyone that has had any celebrity status. Unless you count Carter because he was popular with all the flight attendants. "That makes sense. What do you do when you are recognized?"

Now, he sets the menu down and looks into my eyes. "When it happens, I wait to see what they're going to do. Sometimes it is to talk or take a picture. Other times they will come up to me and ask for an autograph."

That has got to be annoying. I don't know that I would ever get used to that kind of life. "Do you usually give them one?"

"Yeah, usually. It won't do me any good to act like an asshole. Besides, it only takes a few seconds for me to sign a piece of paper or whatever they have on them."

So, he's not an asshole. He's just pushy as hell until he gets what he wants. "Do you know what you want?" The only reason I'm asking is to change the subject. This is the first, and most likely only date we will ever have, and I don't need to know his full life story.

"Not really. I mean pizza is pizza, right?"

I set my menu on the table and bring my hands to my chest in surprise. "No, pizza is not pizza. You're in Chicago. One of the best places in the United States to eat pizza."

Bentley leans back and crosses his arms over his chest, "Okay then, which one should I get?" I don't miss the way his shirt tightens over his arm muscles. And it feels like the temperature in here just went up 10°.

"That depends, what sort of things do you like?"

"As much as you probably don't agree, I'm actually a simple guy. Cheese or pepperoni are what I stick to."

While I am shocked by his choices, it seems a little boring. "Okay, you wait here and I'll go order the pizza."

There's a line at the counter, and I walk to the back. As I'm standing there, two women break from the line and head straight toward Bentley. I guess his presence in the small pizzeria didn't go as unnoticed as he hoped. A pang hits as they sit down, exactly where I just vacated, and start a conversation. I wish I could see him. Even if this is only a one-time thing, it hurts that he's talking to other women while he's on a date with me. One of the women leans over the table, showing off her cleavage and I want to do something to let them know he's here with me. I'm not sure where this possessive streak has come from, and I don't know if I like it or not.

Before I do anything drastic, like turn around and stride right out the door, Bentley scoots his chair back. What's he going to do? Leave with the beautiful women by his side? I'm seconds away from leaving, but he surprises me. He's by my side in less than a minute. "Do you want to get out of here?"

I peer over his shoulder and notice the two women staring, wide mouthed. I guess they didn't think he'd walk away from them. "That sounds like a fantastic idea." My pizza craving will have to wait. He left those two who no doubt offered him more than I'm willing to, and now I want to see the layers this man has to be hiding. There's no way he's arrogant and sweet. Or, maybe, he's trying to get more from me that I'm willing to give. Either way, I want to find out.

NINE

Bentley

Sometimes I wonder what is wrong with people. I'm not even that famous. Rookies should not get this much attention. In most cases...they wouldn't. The only reason they even know who I am is because I helped demolish the home team last night.

Those women saw me sitting with Jolene. They were waiting for their opportunity to pounce. I smiled and nodded along to whatever they were saying. I'm almost certain they told me their names, but I forgot them the second they were spoken. Too dumbfounded with their audacity when they could see I was here with someone.

These are the women I usually take home when I'm in Austin. The sort of women Jordan warns me about daily. I've always let it go in one ear and out the other. There was never a reason not to live my life to the fullest. To take advantage of all the perks for being a professional athlete. Until now. Until her.

I could feel Jolene's eyes on me the entire time. If I

didn't do something fast, she'd be gone. My thought was almost a reality when I left the table and saw her turning toward the door. I can't let her see what my life normally is. Not if I want her to give me a chance.

It's a beautiful, but cool day, in Chicago, and I wish I would have brought my jacket. Jolene isn't fazed as she walks down the sidewalk beside me. She must be from a northern state. There's no way anyone from the South could handle this without freezing their ass off. "Where do you want to go now?" Her voice breaks into my thoughts.

"I have no idea. You probably know this city better than I do." She seems more closed off now than she did when she walked into the pizzeria. I know it has to do with the unwelcome table crashers. "Look, I'm sorry about that back there. I was hoping since I'm not in my home city I wouldn't be as recognizable."

"It doesn't help that you played your ass off last night and stomped them," she laughs.

I turn my head toward her, my mouth lifting into a grin. "So, you watched the game last night?"

Shaking her head, she sighs. Busted. "I may have caught the highlights during the news."

"Good to know." She totally watched the game. "I'm kind of surprised you weren't out on the town. The flight landed early."

"I'm not much of a party animal. I spend so much time in the air that I want nothing more than a bed to take a nap. It's one of the things I miss the most."

"Don't you typically get to sleep in an actual bed?" That's such a weird thing to miss.

She shrugs her shoulders, but angles her body closer to mine. Progress, maybe? "Yeah for the most part. But I was doing international flights for a long time and sometimes we'd have to sleep during the flight. Those small cots aren't very comfortable."

I rear back, eyes wide. "I didn't even know planes had beds on them."

"You also don't fly very much." She bumps her shoulder into mine, "You should try flying first class sometime. It's much nicer up there than it is where you've been sitting."

"Do you ever work first class?"

Jolene shakes her head. "Not often. I prefer being in coach. Lana loves working in that area, though."

"Then I don't see a reason for me to sit there." I hold my hand out in the small space between us, hoping she'll take it. One. Two. Three seconds pass before I think she's not going to take it, but then her hand slides into mine. It's soft and smooth against the roughness of my hand. "If I sat in first class, I wouldn't be able to see you."

She stops in her tracks, her hand ripping away from mine, and laughs loud and hard. I'd be surprised if people down the block can't hear her. After a minute she gathers her composure and meets my eyes. "That has got to be the worst line I've ever heard." I open my mouth to protest. I thought it was pretty smooth, but she stopped me. "I'm here, most likely against my better judgement. This is your time to shine and give me an amazing date, not give me cheesy pickup lines."

"It wasn't that bad," I mutter under my breath.

"What was that?" She walks toward me, and I can't stop staring at her legs peeking out from the bottom of her dress. It's not short, but it has just the right amount of appeal. Showing me a little and making me wonder about the rest. She's so different from anyone I'm typically drawn to, and that terrifies me.

"Nothing." I play it off. As if she didn't just deliver a

blow to my ego. Those lines usually work on most women. "Is there anywhere close by where we could eat? It's freezing out here."

"So cold is your weakness. I'll tuck that nugget of information away." Does that mean she'll go on another date with me? She could be softening me up after laughing at me.

"Hey, us Southern boys don't do well in frigid temperatures. If it's less than seventy degrees, there's a good chance I will be wearing a hoodie."

"Yeah, yeah," she waves her hand at me, dismissing my complaint. "There's a small Italian restaurant around the corner. It's usually slower there since it's off the beaten path."

She doesn't seem too upset that we're going somewhere more isolated, and I follow her lead. As much as I want to take her hand again, I don't think she'd let me. I've never met a woman so hard to read. One minute she's putting me in my place and the next she's opening up, letting me see the softer side to her.

Most of the women I've dated are shallow. Even in high school and college. They wanted to be with me for the popularity. I was one of the star players and being on my arm somehow raised their status. Half of them had never even been to my house. They didn't care.

Right now, I don't know which way Jolene is leaning. She was ready to march out on our date because those women talked to me, but was willing to hold my hand when I reached out. It's giving me whiplash, but I'll stay on the rollercoaster a little longer. It'll either be the ride of my life or I'll be stuck in misery. Maybe today I'll have my answer which one it will be.

≈

She wasn't kidding when she said this place is off the beaten path. We turned right at the next corner, but it wasn't where I was expecting it. It's literally a hole in the wall restaurant. We left the heavy foot traffic behind a few minutes ago. A bright neon red open sign is placed in the window by the door. It resembles a breakfast diner, and I'm not so sure it's a place I want to eat. I've had good and bad experiences at those types of restaurants. Most of those times included copious amounts of alcohol. Just because I was a dedicated ballplayer doesn't mean I didn't know how to have a good time.

I open the door, but stay put after she walks inside. She takes a few steps and stops, realizing I'm not behind her. "Are you coming? I thought you were cold."

"Yeah, about that. Is it safe to eat here? It looks kind of sketchy." I peer around her, trying to get a feel for the inside.

Her brows furrow and the happy mood she was in vanishes at my question. "Does it not live up to your 'high class' expectations?"

Fuck. Everything was going great until I had to open my mouth. "It's nothing against this place. I just have issues with new places in general. Especially when I don't know what I'm walking into." Little does she know I've eaten at some horrible looking places, but the food was excellent. I'm officially an asshole. I've been trying to persuade this woman to look past her first thoughts and give me a chance, but yet I can't do the same thing over a simple fucking place to eat.

She walks toward the door, and me. "We don't have to

eat here." She's wearing a smile, but the tone of her voice speaks volumes.

Before she's out the door, I grab her elbow, stopping her from walking away...yet again. "It's fine. I trust you."

"Are you sure about that?" The flash of pain across her face surprises me. I want to know what idiot put that doubt in her mind and do anything in my power to make it better.

"Yes. If you were trying to do something horrible to me, I think you'd come up with something more creative than food poisoning. Especially since you're hungry, too." Right? What crazy person would also eat something they intend to harm another person with?

"I'm not insane. If I didn't want to be here, or with you, I wouldn't have agreed to the date." She pulls her arm out of my grasp, and heads back into the restaurant. I hurry behind her to keep from insulting her.

Is she always this temperamental? I want to say no, but whoever she dated before must have done a number on her. She's leaning on the hostess stand, waiting for her to show up. "So, what would you recommend that I get?" It's a simple question, and one that hopefully won't spark a debate.

"They have pretty much everything an Italian restaurant would normally have, but I'm still in the mood for pizza. And their pizza is to die for."

I'm a little intimidated that she knows of great restaurants in a town she doesn't even live in. I'll take her word for it though, and I'll get the pizza. It's the least I can do after the way I've continuously stuck my foot in my mouth.

A short older lady emerges from a door I assume leads to the kitchen, and as soon as she sees Jolene her face lights up. "How have you been JoJo? I can't remember the last time I saw you. Are you still doing the long flights?"

Jolene hurries to the woman and wraps her up in a hug.

"It's been too long, Marie. And, no, I'm doing mostly US flights right now."

"Where's Lana? She's usually attached to your side." Marie leans around Jolene's, spotting me, and lifts an eyebrow. "I see you've traded her for a man friend. And a good-looking one at that."

Jolene turned toward me and her cheeks are a rosy shade of red. She gestures toward me and says, "This is my friend, Bentley." I don't miss the way she emphasizes friend. I have a new goal, now. Make her refer to me as more than a friend by the end of today. It won't be easy, but I've never been one to back down from a task.

"Hi, Marie. I'm Bentley." I hold out my hand to shake hers.

She waves me off and wraps her arms around me. "Around here, we hug. Especially when it's a friend," she rolls her eyes at the word, "of one of our favorite people."

"You remind me a lot of my mom." That slipped out of my mouth without my permission. That's a great way to portray myself...as a mama's boy. "She's a hugger, too." Maybe that will explain it away. But she reminds me of Mom. She's so welcoming and gives people chances over and over again. She sees the good in everyone, even if they aren't all that great.

"I like you already." She points toward the dining area, "Sit anywhere you want JoJo. We don't have many other guests and we're light on staff today. One of the girl's had a birthday party last night, and I think half the crew went. Needless to say, they're all feeling pretty horrible today."

"Thank you, Marie." Jolene turns toward the tables set off to the side and doesn't wait to see if I follow her.

I'm happy she picked this place. Even though it doesn't look like much from the outside, it has the same vibe as some of my favorite Mexican restaurants in Austin. You feel like you're at home amongst family. A part of me wonders if I'll ever be allowed to call the woman in front of me "JoJo". It seems like a name she only lets a select few call her. I don't even think Lana calls her by that name. At least she didn't the few times I've seen them around each other.

Jolene picks a table next to a window, and it's refreshing being able to sit out in the open without worrying about photos being taken, or people interrupting our lunch. I should have put more trust in Jolene before making an ass of myself.

Marie comes over as soon as we are situated, "What would you like to drink?" Jolene orders a coke and I ask for water. While I'm a huge binge snacker in the off season, I'm relatively healthy when I know I have to be out on the court.

As soon as Marie leaves the table, Jolene is my only focus. "How long have you been coming here to gain such an adorable nickname? Did you used to live here, or something?"

She scrunches her nose at my questions, but doesn't answer them right away. Maybe this is too personal for her and she doesn't want me to know. Marie comes back with our drinks and sets them on the table, winking at me before she returns to her tasks. Jolene takes a sip of her coke and finally answers me. "She is the only person who calls me that. I'm not a big fan of nicknames and the only reason she gets away with it is because she's the sweetest woman I know." Grabbing the napkin from the edge of the table, she tears small pieces off. I make her nervous. "And I've never lived here, but when I first became a flight attendant, I flew into Chicago, a lot. I found this place one time when I got lost and I come here anytime I'm in the area."

"So, you're practically family now?"

She jerks her head back. "How do you know that?"

"If she's anything like my mom, she never meets a stranger, and feels like it's her job to mother anyone she comes into contact with."

"I think I'd like your mom." She picks up her glass to take a drink.

"You could have a chance to meet her," I wink.

Her eyes go wide and she almost spits out her coke. "Woah. That's a little fast." She picks up the napkin she was ripping to shreds and pats her mouth. "You're assuming we'll make it past this date." Marie comes back with a pizza, even though we haven't ordered yet. Jolene must see the confusion on my face because as soon as Marie leaves, she says, "It's the only thing I ever order."

It's a pretty big pizza for two people, but I'm starving and know I'll be able to put a sizeable dent in it. "By the way, I don't have to assume about another date. I know there will be a next one."

"Someone is full of themselves." She gets up to talk to Marie and comes back with two plates. "No more talking. It's time to eat." She grabs a slice of pizza and sets it on her plate. "Trust me, you'll want to eat more than talk once you've had your first bite."

I grab a slice and take a bite before it ever hits my plate. I wonder how many types of cheese Marie used because the flavor explodes in my mouth. The pepperoni is crisp, yet soft, and a moan slips from me. Jolene giggles, "Told you."

And just like that, our conversation has come to a standstill. By the time I'm on my third slice, I'm full. But Jolene... she eats without a care in the world. As much as I don't do relationships, this woman was made for me.

TEN

Jolene

"Did you like it?" Bentley is scooting back from the table. The chair scraping across the floor. We're the only ones in the place, and it feels intimate.

"We may have to get an Uber to get us back to the hotel. I don't think I can move." He pats his stomach and groans. "My next practice will be brutal because of this."

Like he'll have any issue at practice. I, on the other hand, will have to hit up the tiny gym the airport hotel has. "I'm sure it'll be so painful."

"Laugh all you want. I rarely eat like this during the season. Mostly it's grilled food and things I can work off fast." He waves his hand over the table, "Believe it or not, this food really slows me down."

"Do you ever eat comfort food? Or, do you typically only eat health nut food?" I can't imagine having to eat healthy all the time. I have a small stash of snacks all throughout my apartment.

"Sometimes," he shrugs. "I reserve most of that for the

off season, but still only allow myself a small portion. It's all about balance."

"The only thing I balance is a glass of wine in one hand and a cookie in the other."

His mouth opens wide, shocked by my comment. "That doesn't even sound good." He looks around the empty room and nods his head toward the door. "You ready to get out of here?"

"Sure." Part of me wants to stay here, to keep the date going because I want to see if he has any other soft sides. The other part, however, wants to get the hell out of here. That part is smart. Avoid the possibility of feelings and not get sucked in by his charisma. Even though he acted like a complete ass when we got here, he has more to him. I want to know what that is. If we stay here any longer, I'll be pulled further in. I don't have a lifestyle suitable for dating anyone not in my field.

Bentley walks to the hostess stand and pulls out his wallet. Marie is talking animatedly to him, arms flying in every direction, and then she laughs harder than I've ever heard her laugh. What is it with this guy and older ladies? They seem to eat out of the palm of his hand. It's weird. But if Marie is warming up to him, that has to mean something. It took her a while to even interact with Lana, and she's my best friend.

He doesn't come back to the table, so I grab my clutch and head toward them. "You two are mighty chummy. What's so funny?"

"Oh, nothing," Marie waves me off. She pulls me into a hug, "Come back and see me the next time you're in town." Bringing me closer to her, she whispers in my ear, "Be careful with this one. He could be a keeper and he's a smooth talker."

I simply nod and back away from her. Thanks for putting that thought in my head. Any sign of heartbreak, and I'm out. Her comment just sealed the deal on this going any further.

Bentley reaches for my hand, and I debate taking it. I don't want to give him the wrong impression, but his hand felt spectacular earlier. I can't remember the last time I held hands with a man. His are the perfect balance of rough and soft. It almost matches his personality. A hard exterior to hide the soft interior he doesn't want anyone else to see. Too many conflicting feelings. Those emotions don't stop my hand from sliding into his, though.

"A car should be here to pick us up in just a few," he says as we walk toward the door. Then he turns his head toward the stand again. "Marie, I'll be back next time I'm in town. The food was delicious."

"You're welcome back anytime," she calls out. "Good luck on the rest of your season."

"Thank you." He pushes the door open, and a gust of wind hits us. The temperature has dropped since we went inside, and I wrap my free arm around myself to block some of the wind. I'm used to colder temps, but not such a dramatic drop. Hopefully, this doesn't mean there will be wintry weather and we'll be stuck here for longer. I'm ready to sleep in my own bed. "I wish I had a jacket to offer you."

His voice shakes me from thoughts. "I didn't expect it to get so cold."

He pulls out his phone and checks an app. "The driver should pull around soon."

No sooner than the words leave his mouth, a car pulls up to the curb. "Wow. That was fast. How long ago did you set it up?"

"When I went to talk to Marie and pay the bill." He

shakes his head, astonished. "I wish the service was this fast back in Austin. Sometimes you have to wait almost an hour depending on the time of day...and if there is a game happening."

"It's not common here, either. You must be lucky."

He takes his hand out of mine and opens the back door of the car. "After you, Mademoiselle."

I roll my eyes and get in, sliding across the seat until I'm almost touching the other door. "I bet you've been waiting your whole life to use that."

He shrugs, "Not really. It just sounded good." He mutters something else under his breath, but I didn't catch it. Louder he adds, "We can head back to the hotel I'm staying in."

The offer is tempting, but no. I can't do this past today. No more dates, and hopefully he doesn't bug me about it on any more flights we might be on together. "Sorry, I can't." He starts to say something, but I cut him off. "I have plans with Lana." I don't, not really. But I figure it's the easiest way to let him down.

"Okay, I understand that." He looks at the driver. "Can you drop her off at the hotel by the airport then take me to Knight Hotel?"

The driver turns around to face us, "It'll be easier if I drop you off first since your hotel is a lot closer."

"Are you okay with that?" Bentley asks.

Honestly, that works out better. Then there won't be any chance he'll talk his way to my hotel room. I have no doubt that he'll try. "Yeah, that's fine with me."

His face falls, and I can tell I hurt his feelings. "Okay, we'll do that." The car moves forward until we come out of the side street onto one of the main roads. "Maybe we can grab breakfast in the morning."

Damn. Looks like I won't be avoiding this conversation after all. Let's see, how can I do this gently? "I had a great time today, but I don't think it's a good idea for us to go on another date."

"Why not?"

"Because our schedules are insane, and we'd never see each other. Besides, I still don't really know you."

"Isn't dating how you get to know someone?"

He has a point. "I'm just not ready to seriously date someone."

We pull up to his hotel, and I can see the argument bubbling up inside him. "You say that now, but I'm betting you'll go on another date with me. You'll realize you miss my company and want something more than just your bed."

Those words are a shot straight to my heart. He doesn't have to call out my insecurities like that, but I won't back down. "I'm sorry. I just can't."

"Okay," he says as he opens the car door. "I'll see you on the flight in the morning."

"Bye, Bentley." He shuts the car door and I watch him enter the hotel as the car drives away. He was right. One day I will want more. Today is not that day, though. At least, I don't think it is.

Lana is sitting on the bed, her eyes on the door, and a big goofy grin on her face. "I didn't get a save me text, or call. I assume the date went well?"

I groan and toss my bag on the dresser by the door. "Define well."

She jumps up and comes toward me until she's right in front of my face. "I mean, since I didn't get a call, that means you had an excellent time. When's your next date?" It's a wonder she didn't start poking me to get her point across.

Sidestepping around her, I flop on my bed. "There isn't one."

"Oh no," she gasps. "What happened?"

I shrug and my dress rides up. Is it too early to change into yoga pants, climb into bed, and watch Netflix? "Nothing. The date was actually pretty good. There were a few moments when he was an ass, but overall...it was good."

She arches an eyebrow and squints one eye, studying me. "Then why isn't there going to be another date?" She's more invested in this than I am, and I need to find her angle. She's never badgered me about dating as much as she has these past two weeks.

The television is on, and some guy behind a tall desk is droning on about the game last night. An image of Bentley flashes across the screen. Seriously, this has to come on right now? I turn my attention to the ceiling. My focus is safer there. "Because it's not feasible. We don't live in the same place, and we're both constantly traveling. How in the hell would that even work?" I sigh, "there isn't time to date with those schedules. Besides, I'm not ready to date."

"With an attitude like that, you'll never be ready," she snaps. The bed dips beside me, and I know I'm about to get my ass handed to me by my best friend. "Look, you've moped over Carter long enough. It's time to move on." I open my mouth, but she covers it with her hand. "No, you don't get to talk yet." I lick her hand and she snatches it back, wiping it on the bed. "Anyway, you are way too young to turn into a spinster. Go out and live a little. Why do I have to keep having this conversation with you?"

She has a point. Lots of them, actually. But I'm not

telling her that. "Because I'm hard headed and don't listen."
It doesn't lighten the mood like I hoped it would. "I have
trust issues, okay. He's a celebrity figure. If you don't believe
me, look all over the internet. Women throw themselves at
him constantly. Hell, two women did it today when we
were at the pizzeria the second I left the table." I take a deep
breath before continuing. "I haven't exactly had the best of
luck with people sticking by me. My parents got pissed
when I chose this career and I can't remember that last time
I've talked to them. Then Carter ended up being a dud.
Why should I open myself up to that kind of hurt again?"

Lana grabs my arm and pulls me up until I'm sitting.
"First off, your parents suck. You followed your dreams
instead of settling on something that wouldn't make you
happy. Second, you knew what you were getting into with
Carter. That almost ruined our friendship, and as shitty as it
is to say, I'm glad it ended. It wouldn't have lasted, and I
don't know that our friendship would have survived if you
kept it up with him."

"You're right. That's a shitty thing to say. But I knew
deep down it was a short-term thing. I was mostly pissed
that he found his happily ever after not long after we were
over."

"At least you recognize that now." She looks past me to
the television and grabs my chin until I'm facing it. "On the
other hand, that man wants to date you, no matter how
many times you've turned him down."

The picture on the screen is one of him dunking on the
home team. It's no wonder he's gaining popularity as a
rookie. From the few things I've seen, he's really good. "I
don't know if I can handle dating someone that will likely
become high profile. Besides, how long would he actually
date me until someone younger and prettier comes along?"

"When those women threw themselves at him during lunch today, did he engage?"

"No," I pout. He acted like a gentleman, much to my surprise. "But I still don't know." I take my eyes off the screen and turn toward her, "Can we talk about something else? I don't really want to get lost in my feelings. Besides, you're the one who told me to keep it casual with him, and now you're pushing me on him like he's the answer to all my problems."

She shrugs her shoulders and laughs. "What can I say? I like his energy. If there's anyone not scared to argue their point against you, it's him." She looks around the room before focusing on me again. "Since you aren't seeing him and don't want to get all up in your feelings...come drink with me tonight."

"Lana," I protest.

"Hear me out. It'll be a girl's night. It's been forever since we've hung out and drank together."

"We literally did that a few days ago." It was probably the most relaxing time I've had in a while. We had wine, did facemasks...the whole shebang.

"I mean one where we leave the hotel." She stands up and heads to her suitcase. "I won't even try to dress you. For all I care, you can wear yoga pants and a sweatshirt. I just know I need out of this hotel room. I'm not meant to be cooped up."

"You've had all day to leave. Why didn't you go anywhere?"

"I wanted to be here in case you needed me. What kind of friend would I be if I bailed on you to go on a shopping trip?"

"I honestly don't know how you fit all your shopping spree items into your suitcase. I'm beginning to think it's magical." She really is an amazing friend. Hell, my parents pretty much cut me off when I told them I wanted to travel the world. But this woman, who isn't even my blood, stayed here just in case the date was a disaster. "And I'll go out with you tonight. Don't expect me to go all crazy, though. Our flight still leaves at a decent time."

"Yay," she squeals. "I'll go get ready. We can grab dinner then head to a bar."

"Sounds good. I'm going to go change into something more comfortable." I point to the dress in question. "It won't take me long."

"We're going to have so much fun." She rushes to the bathroom to begin her "going out" ritual. She's the only one that can drag me out, even if I don't feel like it. I'm just happy I'll always have her in my corner. My life would be boring without her crazy antics. As for my dating life...that can wait for another day. Tonight, is all about me and my bestie.

ELEVEN

Bentley

"WHAT DO you mean she declined a second date?" Jordan asks over the phone. He and his wife left for the airport about an hour ago. Announcements can be heard in the background, and it only reminds me of Jolene.

"Exactly what I said." I run my fingers through my hair and sigh. "I thought everything was going great. I asked for a second date, and she threw out every excuse in the world to turn it down."

"I know you don't want to hear this, but she might be a lost cause." He mumbles something, I'm assuming to his wife, before he speaks again. "As much as I hate saying this, you're probably better off dating girls the way you have been. Even if it's something I don't agree with."

"But I can't get her out of my head." Frustration doesn't even begin to cover what I'm feeling, and you can see the path I've paced in the hotel's carpet. "I don't even know why. It's not like I even know her. She caught my attention on the flight and has stayed in my thoughts since then. What is wrong with me? This isn't normal."

"Dude, there isn't anything wrong with you." He pauses for a beat, then laughs. "Except for the fact you're a pushy asshole."

"That's not helping." I need to get this girl out of my system.

"Why don't you see who's still there and see what they're doing tonight?"

"You know damn well most of the team doesn't like me." They talk to me at practices and games. That's it.

"Because you're a cocky rookie. You need to earn their respect instead of running up and down the court acting like you're better than them."

"I am better than most of them." I sit on the sofa. Yep, there's a sofa in the hotel room. That was a new thing for me. If it wasn't for me showing up last night, we would have lost that game.

"That doesn't matter. We are a team. You seemed to have forgotten what that's like considering you just graduated from college." He sighs, and I can imagine him shaking his head. He does that a lot where I'm concerned. "You need to hang out with them outside of games and really get to know them. Maybe by showing them you aren't a jackass; they'll like you better."

"Okay," I drawl. "And what am I supposed to do after I see who's still here."

"Go out and get a drink with them. Hang out with them. You'll be working on your relationship with them and getting your mind off the girl. Two birds, one stone."

He has a point. It'd be nice to actually fit in with the team for once. To be a part of the group without feeling like I don't belong. It's not that I need their approval. Not exactly. It'll be nice to not have to hear the shitty remarks they have about me being on the team. They've had years to build their friendships. "Okay, I think I can do that."

"Good." His wife says something but I can't hear her over the airport noise. "I have to go. But get out and have fun tonight. If that means finding a woman to hang out with, so be it. Just don't do anything more. We need your head in the game and not on a one-night stand."

"It hasn't screwed up my game yet."

"You know what I mean. I'll catch you back in Austin." He hangs up before I can say anything else.

"Asshole," I mutter. How am I supposed to get a hold of anyone to hang out with? Knock on their doors like a little kid asking if they want to come out and play? Maybe Jordan's plan isn't such a great idea. Staying in my room, moping, sounds like a much better idea.

Damn, is this what I've turned into? I barely even know this woman, and I'm freaking out over her denying one date with me. This is stupid. I think I'm going to take my team-mates' advice and live it up tonight. It's a shame those two women from the pizzeria didn't slip me their phone numbers. But I was trying to be respectful of my date and walked away from them before they had a chance to do anything.

I scroll through my phone to see whose phone number I have. It's not many, and I'm debating whether this is a good idea or not. This woman has made me start second guessing myself, and that's something I've never done. At least, not since dad walked out on us when I was eight years old. I was always worried I wasn't good enough, or asked myself what I did to make him leave. But I never came up with an answer. And that is why I just don't become attached to people. The only people who have never let me down are my mom, my sister, my coaches, and my teammates.

Well, until now at least. I don't think half of my teammates even like me, and that is something I will change starting now.

A knock comes from my door, scaring the hell out of me, and I drop my phone on the floor. "Shit, I hope I didn't just shatter the screen."

I pick up the phone before standing up and heading toward the door. Thank God there's not even so much as a scratch, but I have no idea who would show up at my door right now. It can't be any ball chasers because the hotel is under strict guidelines not to give out that information. Not that they would anyway, but our owners like to make sure they know not to. I open the door and come face to chest with one of my teammates. "Ross, what are you doing here?" The question comes out more aggressive than I intend, and I slap myself on the forehead. "Sorry, come on in."

Ross ducks his head and comes through the door before shutting it behind him. You never realize how much taller your teammates are until you're no longer on the court. "Jordan mentioned you might need someone to chill with tonight, and I figured I'd ask if you wanted to come down to the hotel bar and drink a few with me."

I guess Jordan knows me better than I thought. I may think I'm better than most of the people on my team, but I also don't like confrontation. At least, unless it includes a feisty brunette in a flight attendant uniform. "Yeah, that actually sounds pretty good."

"You might want to change. You look like you've been sleeping in those clothes, and as much as I don't think you will be bothered, you should always dress to impress when out in the public eye." He walks back to the door and opens it, "Is an hour enough time? I'll just meet you down there to make things easier."

"Sure, an hour should be plenty of time."

He doesn't say anything else and walks out the door. Come to think of it, he doesn't say much at practice either. But he has the respect of our entire team and I'm glad he is the one Jordan reached out to.

Looks like I'll need to see what else is in my suitcase if I'm going to be presentable. The funny thing is, Jordan has never once mentioned anything like that. I have zero doubts it's because he doesn't want my ego to go to my head even more than it already does. Oh well, tonight my ego is all I have.

Ross is leaning against the bar when I walk into the dimly lit room. He's chatting to the bartender, but it's not the same one from last night. This bartender has long blonde hair and her shirt is unbuttoned just enough for her cleavage to tease the male customers. That woman knows how to draw them in, and I shake my head. I have a feeling Ross isn't leaving here alone tonight. Not if the wide blue eyes staring at him from the other side of the bar top are any indication.

He doesn't notice me until I'm sliding into the barstool next to him. "Can I get a Crown and Coke?"

The bartender bats her eyes at him and then turns to me, "Sure thing."

"Damn," Ross mutters. "That girl is so fucking hot."

"I'm sure she feels the same about you," I laugh. The sports channel is on the small television in the corner again, and it's playing whatever game is on tonight. I don't pay too much attention. At least, not right now. When I get home tomorrow, I'll be glued to the screen, taking notes on what the players are doing. It's smart to keep an eye on other teams. It's the only way to get better.

The bartender sets my drink in front of me, and a small grin crosses her lips as she eyes Ross. "If you need anything else, just let me know."

"Thanks," I say.

"So, I hear you're trying to heal a broken heart." He takes a long sip of his drink before setting it on the counter and pushing it back and forth between his hands. I wish he'd sit down. He's taller than me when we're both standing, and now it feels like I'm talking to a giant.

"I think Jordan talks too damn much." I grimace at my glass. Did he have to tell him anything? How in the hell was there even time? Unless...he somewhat set this up before he left. I wouldn't put it past him. He seems to know what's going on with my life before I do. It must be because he's 'older and wiser' or whatever. He's not even that much older than me and already acts like a grandpa.

"Is it a broken heart?" He finally sits down on the barstool and spreads his legs out so his knees don't hit the counter. "I'm not one to judge, but the best medicine is to find a night of fun."

"You know, I think this is the most I've heard you talk since I signed onto the team." He shakes his head but doesn't say anything, waiting me out until I'll answer his question. Fine. I'll do it only because I want to talk about something, anything, else. "Not really a broken heart. I've only seen the woman a handful of times. She got under my skin and bruised my ego, though."

"That's tough, man. You can't let the females get you down." He takes another sip of his drink. "I'm sure there are plenty of women in here tonight that wouldn't mind warming your bed."

I'm not looking for a bed warmer. I just want to get my mind off Jolene for a while. Seeing her on the plane ride back home tomorrow will be a punch to the gut. I wonder if it's too late to upgrade my ticket to first class. No. I'll sit in my seat and act like her rejection meant nothing. Fake it until you make it, right? "Honestly, this is helping. I don't hang out with much of the team."

"That's because you're arrogant as hell," he slaps my shoulder, almost knocking me off my stool. Son of a bitch, remind me not to get on his bad side. If that was a playful push, imagine what he could do if he fought anyone. "Nobody wants to hang out with someone like that."

"Then why don't you go out with the guys?" It's a genuine question, I've never seen him in any of the local tabloids.

"Because my mama would kick my ass if she thought I was causing trouble." He shakes his head as if he's ashamed of fearing his mom. I get it. My mom is one of the kindest women I know, but if she actually picked up any of the trash magazines, she'd give me a good ass whipping. "I do the same things the rest of them do, but I keep a low key."

"That's smart," I agree. "I do too, except I'm by myself."

"Dude, don't even lie. I've seen the pictures online. You always have some hot chick hanging on your arm."

"Yeah, and they usually get pissed off when I send them packing the next morning."

"That's because they're looking for a payload. They don't give a damn about you, just their fifteen minutes in the limelight." He's not telling me anything I don't know. He glances up at the television screen and nods. "How do you think we'll do against them?"

I pick up my glass and take another long pull. At the rate I'm going, I'm going to need another one pretty soon. "It'll be a win, easy. We just have to watch their defense. They don't like—" I pause with my drink halfway to the counter at the sound of her voice. What the fuck is she doing here?

"They don't like what?" Ross has no idea that the reason for my mood just walked into the bar.

I hold my finger up and tilt my head to hear what they are saying. Of all the places they could go in this city, and they come here.

"He's probably out with his teammates. I don't know why you're worried." Lana's voice is loud and captures Ross's attention.

"Because, I basically told him I didn't have time for him. Why did you pick this place, anyway?"

I want to turn around. I want to see her, but I don't. I stay perfectly perched on my stool, waiting to see what else they are going to say.

"Hey man, is that her?" Ross whispers.

"Shhh."

Lana finally answers, "It's the only place that doesn't care about casual clothes and the drinks are reasonably priced."

"I swear, Lana, if he's here, I will smack you." She's quiet for a minute. "I'm regretting coming out with you."

"Oh, get over yourself," Lana admonishes her. "It's not like you can avoid him forever. In case you don't remember, he'll be on the flight in the morning."

They walk around the bar into my line of sight. I duck my head so they can't see me, but I can still see them. They head to the opposite side of the room, and I can no longer hear them.

"Son of a bitch. Do I have some sort of unlucky sign attached to my back?"

Ross laughs and smacks his hand on the bar top. "That was the funniest shit I've ever seen. I don't think I've ever seen your face that pale."

"Shut up, asshole," I grumble. "I can't believe she's here. It's like Fate is fucking taunting me."

"You know, you could always just go talk to her?" He points in the direction they went. "She's literally sitting right over there."

"Because being rejected a second time in one day is such a great idea." I tap my finger against my chin. "Why didn't I think of that before?"

Ross waves his hand to grab the bartender's attention. "It's not that bad. Like I said before. There are plenty of women out there who would kill to go on one date with you. Why are you losing your shit over one you barely even know?"

"I don't know, man. That's the part I can't figure out." I gaze in the direction they went. "There's just something about her. She's not like any other woman I've met before. She also isn't afraid to call me on my shit. I think that might be one of the biggest things."

"You mean that's all we have to do during practice? Tell you to stop fucking up, and you'll lose your ego?" He's smiling, and that's the only sign he's joking. The bartender finally comes to our side, and before she can say anything he says, "Hey, Honey, can we get another round?" She nods, and he adds, pointing at me, "Make his, a double. He needs it."

If he keeps plying me with alcohol, I'll be lucky to make it to the airport on time in the morning. Changing the subject, I point to the television screen, "Back to what I was saying earlier, we have to watch their defense. They stick to you like glue with man on man."

"That wasn't smooth at all, but I'll allow it."

I'm going to sit right here, get drunk, and act like she's not in the room. It's all I can do at this point. Luckily, I have Ross to keep me distracted.

TWELVE

Jolene

If Lana wanted the ambience of a hotel bar, we could have gone downstairs to the one at the hotel we're staying in. I don't trust her intentions. She's been pushing Bentley on me since the first day I met him and I have a feeling she has some ulterior motives behind all this.

Her eyes are wandering through the bar, not looking for anything in particular, but taking in the vibe. Maybe she really does like this place. It's not somewhere I'd normally venture. I tend to hit the small venues. She somehow finds a way to hang out with the upper echelon when we're in new locations. I tap her arm until her eyes meet mine. "Why are we really here?"

She looks away, no longer interested in making eye contact. Busted. She's never had a problem calling me on my crap, and I'm not going to make things easy for her now. "What do you mean? I already told you why I decided this was a good place."

"I know that," I roll my eyes. "But tell me, to my face,

that it had nothing to do with a certain basketball player. Because I know for a fact that this very hotel is the one he's staying in."

She stares at her hands and mumbles, "It has nothing to do with Bentley."

"What was that? I didn't quite hear you." She's such a liar.

She grabs her drink, placing the straw between her bright red lips, and takes a long pull. I know the action for what it is, her stalling mechanism. She does it every time we drink together, and she doesn't want to answer a question. "Okay, fine," she sets the glass on the table. "I know the team is staying here. I overhead one of the super tall guys mention it in the first-class cabin yesterday." She points her finger at me for the second time today. She's making a habit of that, and I'm not sure that I like it. "But you need to get over your trust issues and give him a chance. I figured if we came here, there might be a chance we'd see him in passing."

"And what? You thought I'd fall into his arms?" It's ridiculous she'd even consider that. "You watch too many movies. Shit like that doesn't happen in real life."

"You never know it might," she argues and takes another drink. "If you'd just date the guy, I wouldn't have to come up with outlandish ways to get the two of you in the same room. It's tiring, honestly." She throws her hands up in the air, not at all amused by the way I've handled things with Bentley.

"I told you earlier that I can't date him. Why do you keep pushing it?" A guy at a table catty corner is eying us. Were we talking too loud? He doesn't look annoyed, but his attention skeeves me out.

"It's not that you can't. You won't. There's a difference."

She grabs her glass but doesn't take a drink. "And I'm pushing it because I need you to be happy. There's no point in you moping around like you just lost your best friend. You know? Because I'm right here. If shit ends badly, I'm always going to be here to help pick you up."

"You're also the one pushing me into something I'm not sure I want. That also makes you a bad choice maker. Best intentions or not."

"I'll gladly wear that title," she grins. "My terrible choices have led to some fun times. You can't deny that." She's not lying. Some of my favorite memories include her leading the way into some horrible idea. It was fun, though. I wish I could be more like her. Throw all caution to the wind and not worry about making an ass of myself.

The man staring at us earlier leaves his table and strides to our table. Even from here I can see his predatory gaze. Warning bells go off in my head, but I don't say anything to Lana. I'm the queen of avoiding confrontation and she'll know how to handle this. She's had far more expertise in this area than I have. He pulls a chair from the table beside us and slides it to the end of ours. He plops into it and rests his arms on the table, leaning toward us. "How are you ladies doing tonight?"

My mouth hangs wide open at the audacity of this man. He has zero tact, and his presence makes me uncomfortable. Lana doesn't skip a beat, though. She eyes him warily before pasting a smile on her face. "We're just fine." Her voice drips with honey and sarcasm. I've always wondered how she does that. She's condescending, and this moron doesn't even realize it.

"Any chance I can buy you ladies a drink?" His gaze shoots to me, and my insides recoil.

"We're perfectly capable of buying our own drinks,

thanks." Lana replies and nods her head toward the bar. I guess that means she wants me to go get the bartender, or at least, someone to help us. She speaks again to get his attention off of me. "We'd much rather be alone, though. We're having a girl's night."

"That's nice," he smirks. "But don't those usually mean you're at home in your pajamas and putting crap on your face?"

"Sometimes. But not tonight." Her voice is louder, hoping to attract anyone's attention. My eyes rove around the room, but it's not as busy as it was when we walked in. Almost all the patrons on this side of the room are gone, leaving us on our own.

"You should end your night early and come hang out with me. What do you say?" Is this guy serious? Lana just told him we want to be alone, and he isn't getting the hint. What the fuck is wrong with some men? I slide out of my seat and stand. If he's not going to get a clue, then I'll find someone here who will make him. We should have sat at the front of the bar. This probably wouldn't be happening if we were closer to people, instead of one of the darkest corners of the room.

I take a step, and his hand snakes out, grabbing my arm. "Where are you going, sweetheart? We're just talking."

My blood is boiling. While I've had no problem going back and forth with Bentley, it's different this time. This man isn't anything like Bentley. Not once have I ever felt like I was in any danger with the basketball player. But the man who invited himself to our table? That's a different story. Just from our small interaction, he is definitely one of those guys you hear about on the news. "Please, let go of my arm."

"Sit down, and I'll let go. Like I said, we're just talking

and getting to know each other." His grip on my arm tightens, and I try to pull away.

I raise my voice much louder than is necessary. "If we are just talking, you have no reason to keep me from leaving the table. Now, let go of me."

Lana shakes her head the slightest bit, a warning to keep my cool because we don't know what this man is capable of. I'm about to pull my arm out of his grasp, once again, but her eyes go wide.

A deep voice sounds from behind me, "Sir, you should probably do what the lady asked." My heart flutters at the sound of his voice, and as much as I hate to admit it, I'm happy he showed up.

"This is none of your business. You should go back to wherever you came from and leave us be."

"You have two options, let her go...or I'll make you."

The man holding onto me sneers as he eyes Bentley up and down. "You seriously think your scrawny self can make me do anything?"

"When it comes to you harassing my friends, I'll do anything in my power to make sure they are safe." He touches my shoulder, letting me know he's behind me, and my body relaxes the tiniest bit at the contact.

The man laughs, and his grasp loosens the tiniest fraction. "You and what army?"

"I don't need an army, but my friend here," he jerks his thumb over his shoulder and a much larger shadow falls over us. "He's not too keen on people manhandling women either." The man in question says and his voice is deep, "Where I come from men don't manhandle women to get what they want."

Suddenly, my arm is free and I pull it toward me as if I'm nursing a wound. "Thank you."

The stranger pushes back his chair and takes a step back, "I'll just go."

"That's probably a good idea. But you should probably just leave the bar because I've already informed the waitress to keep an eye out, and I'm certain she's already called hotel security." The man's face is red as he throws cash down on the table he was at and hurries out of the bar.

Bentley turns me around and bends down until our eyes meet. "Are you okay?"

Even though he only had his hands on me for a couple of minutes, it feels like it's been hours. "Yeah, I'm fine." That doesn't mean I won't have nightmares about that guy practically forcing himself on me, even though he only grabbed my arm.

"Good," he says. "As soon as I realized you walked in, I had the bartender keep an eye on you."

"You've been here the entire time?" What the hell? He had every opportunity to come to me, and the fact that he knew I was here and said nothing it's kind of creepy, but also, not that surprising. "Why didn't you say anything?"

He shrugs, "I don't know. You were here with your friend, and you made it perfectly clear earlier that you didn't have any interest in me bugging you again."

That might be one of the few times my words come back to bite me in the ass. "Well, thank you for coming to my rescue. I'd like to say that we could've handled it, but that guy was worse than any other unwanted attention we've gotten."

"Yeah, usually my pitchy voice gets them to go away, and that guy...he just wasn't having it." Lana comes up to my side and bumps my shoulder. "I honestly don't know what he would have been capable of. So, thank you for me to."

"I seriously hate guys like that. His mama definitely didn't teach him any manners." That comes from the guy standing beside Bentley.

"Hi, I'm Jolene," I hold my hand out to shake his hand.

He steps around Bentley and wraps me in a hug. "I'm, Ross. It's kind of crappy that these are the circumstances we're meeting under." He takes a step back and shakes his head. "Sorry, I just said I don't like dudes who overstep their bounds and I just went in for a hug. That would also be my mom's fault. She's a hugger."

I laugh, "It's fine. You don't give off creepy abductor vibes."

Lana waves at him, "Are you going to be on our flight tomorrow?"

"Of course, I have to see my favorite flight attendant." He gives her a wink and her cheeks reddened.

We all stand there awkward and silent for a minute, and Lana nods her head to the bar, "So do you want to go grab a drink?" Bentley's teammate nods, and he and Lana leave Bentley and I to our own devices.

I gestured to the seat behind me, "At this point, it would be kind of rude if I didn't invite you to sit."

"Thanks." He rounds the table and takes the seat Lana was previously sitting in. "I would have been over here sooner, but by the time the bartender came back around, you had already started raising your voice."

"That is an experience I never want to have again. I knew I should have just stayed in the hotel room tonight."

"But if you did that, I wouldn't have had the opportunity to rescue the damsel in distress."

"So, do you have some kind of hero complex I don't know about? First you stepped in with my awkward conversation without me asking, and now this?"

The bartender comes over and sets fresh glasses on the table. "Those are on the house."

"Thanks," Bentley says. He turns his focus on me, "neither one of these situations was something I planned on. I'm just happy I came down to the bar with my teammate tonight. Otherwise, that could've gone a completely different direction."

"Believe me, I'm grateful." I take a sip of my drink and look around the room, doing anything I can to keep my gaze off the man who continually comes to my rescue and surprises me.

"I guess that means you'll be going on a second date with me."

I spit out the drink I just took, and it goes all over him. "Where in the hell would you get that idea?"

"Well, I know you have an interest in me. Otherwise, you wouldn't be fighting your feelings so hard. Second, I did just rescue and I think that's deserving of a date."

Yet, he continuously surprises me. As much as my encounter a few moments ago rattled me, I'm not going to let that interfere with the rest of my night. He's right. I do have some kind of feelings for him, and before that douche nozzle interrupted my girl's night, I was going to tell Lana that I'm done fighting her, and am willing to take a chance on him. But is now the time to tell him that? I mean, he did bring it up so his mind is obviously in that space. You can do this Jolene, be more like Lana, take life by the horns and see where it leads you. "I don't know, I feel like a second date might not be enough to show you how grateful I am."

His face lights up, and I don't think I've seen him this happy. At least, not since that first time he flew, and we landed at the airport.

"This isn't a joke, is it?" He points at me, "because if it is, you are a cruel woman."

I laugh. "No, it's not a joke. I'm willing to let you attempt to sweep me off of my feet."

"There'll be no attempt," he reaches across the table and places his hand on top of mine. "Before long you won't be able to get enough of me. Mark my words."

Just like that he's thrown down the gauntlet and I know my heart will be his whether I like it or not.

THIRTEEN

Bentley

Ross and I are in the elevator on the way up to our rooms. I'd like to say we closed the hotel bar down, but Lana and Jolene were still pretty shaken up by that asshole. We called them an Uber and sent them back to their hotel. I swear, if I see that guy around the hotel, I'm going to pummel him. He's lucky I even gave him the opportunity to leave the bar. I'm not a violent man, but he didn't have any good intentions, and I'm grateful I was in there tonight. Who knows what would have happened otherwise?

"Dude, no wonder you're head over heels for that chick. She's hot." Ross backs out of the open doors. "You should have seen your face when her voice got loud. You went into defender mode."

"It's not just because she's hot," I roll my eyes at him and follow him out of the elevator. "She's incredibly stubborn. And I'm sure you would have, too. It sure as hell didn't take you long to come up beside me."

"It was in case you needed backup, man. And my mom would also kick my ass if I didn't stand up to defend a lady's honor."

"All I'm hearing is you're scared of your mom." I walk backward toward my room.

"You would be, too." He turns to the opposite end of the hallway but stops. "Next time Mom has a cookout or get together; you're welcome to come. Then you can tell me you aren't scared of her."

"I'm sure she's as sweet as pie."

"Yeah, okay." He turns back toward his room and walks away. "I'll see you at the airport in the morning," he calls over his shoulder.

I stop walking backward, turning until I'm facing the doors on either side of the hallway. As soon as I get to my room, I slide the keycard into the slot and walk in. Before I make it to my suitcase to change into some sleep pants, my phone dings.

Jolene: We made it. Thank you again.
Bentley: No problem. What time do you usually get to the airport? Maybe we can grab breakfast.
Jolene: I'm there a hell of a lot earlier than you are.
Bentley: That sounds like you're neglecting our second date.
Jolene: Calm down. I'm still going on that date with you, just not in the morning.
Bentley: K. Good night. Dream about me. ;)
Jolene: Goodnight dork.

Tossing my phone on the bed, I rummage through my suitcase for my joggers. Even though tonight had a great ending, I'm feeling buzzed from my confrontation with that jerk and need to take a shower to calm myself down. It's almost the same adrenaline that gets me going while I'm on the court, but not quite.

The tile on the bathroom floor is cold against my feet, and I wish places had heated floors. This Texas guy isn't used to everything being so chilly. I turn the handle on the shower until the water warms and steam fills up the bathroom. The only way this shower would feel better is if Jolene had stayed the night with me. I knew she wouldn't agree to that, it's just not in her wiring. Asking her after what happened tonight would definitely lose me points. But a guy can dream.

I step under the hot water and close the shower door behind me. Rather than picturing Jolene's distress tonight, I focus on how she looked this afternoon. How carefree she seemed to be at the Italian restaurant. How her hand felt in mine. And how I wish I could feel it against my skin right now. Soft and hesitant as it slides down my chest before grabbing hold of my cock. Her fingers rubbing small circles over the tip and sliding down until I'm hard as a rock. Fuck, I can't get this girl out of my head. My hand pumps faster and faster. A groan escapes my lips as I come, and I lean forward, resting against the side of the wall.

That shouldn't have happened so fast. I'm already sprung after one date with this woman, and there's no telling what will happen during our next date. All I know is it's been way too long since I've gotten laid, and by the time she lets me inside her, I'm not sure how long I'll be able to last.

~

Even though Jolene said she didn't want to do breakfast, I still get to the airport earlier than necessary. Ross groaned into the phone this morning when I called asking if he wanted to ride together. I believe his exact words were "get bent." So, I'm on my own. Thank God, Jordan showed me what needed to be done on the last two flights, otherwise I'd be screwed.

Getting through security was a breeze. And now I'm sitting outside of my gate, wondering if I'll see the woman who has captured my attention. Do flight attendants even use the same methods we do to get into the airport? Or do they have a super secret entrance only they are allowed to enter? Either way, my eyes are peeled.

Considering the early hour, there are quite a few people boarding planes and getting off them. Families are rushing to make their flights, making sure everyone is accounted for. Men in suits flying back in for their jobs. At least, that's what I'm assuming. We never went anywhere if we couldn't drive. Mom isn't a huge fan of planes and we never really had the money for extravagant trips. I think I'll take her and my sister on a nice vacation after the season is over. Who knows? Maybe Jolene will still be around.

Woah there, buddy. You've gone on one date with this chick. It's too early to be planning for the future. That's making some huge assumptions that I'm not even ready to face. Remember, you don't do relationships, Bentley. She'll end up leaving just like Dad.

"Yo, man. Have you been sitting here the whole time?" Ross's voice scares the hell out of me.

"What time is it?"

"Our flight should start boarding soon. You good?"

Holy shit, I didn't realize I was in my head for so long. I guess I'm getting better at tuning out the noise in this place. Or, maybe you're too busy planning a future you have no business planning. A small part of my subconscious whispers. I'm not, though. This is just for fun. Jolene said she didn't have time for relationships so we'll just hang out when we can, and that will be it.

"Yeah, I'm good. Just hoping to see Jolene before we board."

"You got it bad for this broad." He sees my glare and laughs. "It's all good, though. You do what you gotta do. I'll try not to tease you for it...much."

"Asshole," I mutter.

"What's the word on her friend? After hanging out with her at the bar last night, she seems like a pretty cool chick."

"Oh, I see how it is. You mock me then ask me about her friend." I gaze around the gate, hoping to catch sight of the women in question. "I have no idea. She helped me cross paths with Jolene. Even gave me her flight schedule so I could book flights when she's working. She seems pretty gung-ho on her friend finding someone to spend time with."

"That's all good for you," he leans back into the seat, crossing his ankle over his leg. "But what about her? I'd be lying if I said she didn't catch my attention on previous flights. But I think she's a natural flirt, and shouldn't take trying to hook up with her seriously."

"I don't know. You'll have to ask her yourself."

A voice comes over the intercom, "Now seating first class."

"Looks like I'm heading in. Want me to send a message if I see your girl?"

"She isn't really my girl," I fire back. What the hell has gotten into me? "Sorry, I'm good. I'll see her when I board."

Since coach boards last, I wait until almost nobody else is in line. I don't want to be rushed when I see her. Finally, the people in front of me move forward and my palms are clammy. Before I get too close to the door, I whip my backpack around and pull out a small trinket.

The passengers in front of me are slowly making their way onto the plane, and I feel like a moron with a junior high crush holding this thing in my hands. I'm hoping she thinks it's adorable instead of completely insane.

Finally, I see her brown hair through the line of people. I'm getting closer to her with each step, and I debate throwing the gift on the floor. Acting as if it never existed. Instead, I keep my eyes glued to her and the moment she sees me...her eyes light up and a smile overtakes her face. Relief washes through me. She seems to be as caught up in the chemistry we have as I am.

"Hey," she breathes once I'm in front of her. "When I didn't see you board earlier, I was wondering if you switched flights."

"And miss a chance to see a beautiful face? That's not happening." I wonder if I should tell her how Lana helped me, but I figure if Lana wanted her to know, she'd tell her.

"You got the second date with me, no need to be cheesy."

Well, that withers the bravado I had about giving her a gift. If she thought that was cheesy, there's no way in hell she will accept this without laughing her ass off. "Please, you just wish you had lines like me."

She rolls her eyes. I fumble with my backpack and suitcase, almost dropping the trinket on the floor. Her eyes catch on it, and she reaches for my hand. "What's that?"

"Well, it was a gift for you, but I'm not so sure now. I don't want to be too cheesy."

"Oh, shut up and hand it over." This is why Jolene caught my eye in the first place. She may seem quiet and demure, but she's also demanding. If my mom were here to see this, she'd call her my perfect match. As if that actually exists.

I hand it over and watch as she tries to figure out what it is. I don't make her wait long for an explanation. "It's a paper flower. I know you're not home much, so real flowers were out of the question. This is just something to remind you of our next date. I want to be on your mind every time you see it."

"I'm not sure if I should be offended or not," she laughs. "It's a thoughtful gift, but the fact that you think you're forgettable is funny." She slaps her hand over her mouth at the slip. It's good to know that I cross her mind more than she wants to admit.

"We should catch that date after we land in Austin."

A flash of regret crosses her face. "I can't. I have a back-to-back flight."

Damn it. "We're going to have to figure out this schedule issue. I'm going to need more than a couple of hours after each flight. Especially if you're going to fall head over heels."

"There you go assuming again," her lips quirk into a smirk. "I promise you'll get your date, and we'll make it happen. We'll just have to get creative." She winks and I can't help the wicked thoughts that flitter through my head.

"I can get creative," I wink back.

"You better get seated; we'll be departing soon."

I lean over and give her a quick peck on the cheek. It's less than I want to do, but I have a suspicion she'd smack me if I went in for an actual kiss. "See you in the aisle."

Another eye-roll before I search for an available seat.

Almost all the ones where I normally sit are taken, and I'm kicking myself for not boarding sooner. It was worth it, though. I grab a seat close to the back of the plane and put my suitcase in the overhead storage. I'm going to spend the whole flight thinking of creative ways we can date from afar.

FOURTEEN

Jolene

My phone pings with a message. It's too early in the morning to be dealing with people. And...it's my day off. My feet don't have to leave the ground for three days. I can't even remember the last time I've had such a long break. Usually it's off one day and back in the air the next. I'm not one to look a gift horse in the mouth, though.

I roll over and pull the pillow over my head, as if that will block out everything. No such luck. My phone sends the reminder ping right before it rings. Panic at the Disco, blares through the room. I really need to remember to put that thing on silent before I go to bed. There's only one person who calls me, and it's too early for her to even be up yet. Unless it's an emergency. Or work, and that's the only reason I don't want to answer it. Just in case they are calling me to cover for one of the other attendants. Shit, I better get whatever this is over with.

I reach to the nightstand, my hand knocking over the glass of water I set there last night, until my fingers grasp the phone. I answer it before it goes to voicemail, not bothering to check to see who it is. "Hello, Lana?"

"Guess again." Bentley's voice comes through the speaker and I can envision the smirk he's wearing right this second.

"Ugh, why are you calling so early?" As much as I want to lie down while finding out the reason for his call, I can't. The water I knocked over is dripping onto the floor, and each drop that hits the floor is a soft, but annoying, plop.

"I just finished my workout and thought I'd call you so we can figure out our date." He doesn't even sound out of breath. Who the hell works out and then carries on a conversation like they aren't gasping for air? "I take it you aren't a morning person?"

I swing my legs over the bed and sit up. "Not even a little bit." My feet land in the small puddle of water. Groaning, I do a weird limp walk to the bathroom to get a towel, trying not to get water all over the floor.

"Are you okay? Maybe I should call back later."

"No," I sigh. "You're fine. I spilled a cup of water when I reached for my phone. And I stepped in it."

"Shit," he mutters. "I'm so sorry. I didn't intend to make your morning start off badly."

"It's all good. Nothing a towel can't clean up." Wait, he's calling for information about our second date. How is that even going to happen when we are states apart? Last time I checked when we need to be in the same vicinity to go on one. "You were saying something about the second date? You realize we aren't in the same area, right? Unless you somehow found out where I live and you're stalking me. Which, by the way, is kind of creepy."

He laughs, and I can't help the way my body tingles when I hear the sound. It's deep and full of life. When's the last time I laughed like that? With complete abandon? Oh yeah, on our first date. He seems to bring out another side of me. "No, I'm not stalking you. Though, if I knew the area you were in, this would be a lot easier."

"Yeah, probably." I grab a towel from the shelf and wipe off my foot before heading back into the bedroom to mop up the rest of the mess.

"So, are you going to tell me?" His voice doesn't hold any frustration. "I can always FaceTime you and try to figure it out."

I glance down at the threadbare t-shirt I'm wearing with bleach spots all over it after a laundry incident. My hands go up to my hair, and I can feel the tangles as I try to run my fingers through it. "That's going to be a negative. On the video call, not the other part. I live in Missouri."

"Hm." That's his only response.

"What does that mean?" That makes me a little self-conscious. I'm not from here, but I didn't think it was a horrible place to live.

"Oh, nothing. It's just not where I pictured you'd be living."

"Where did you think I live?" I'm kind of offended. Does my accent give off a certain vibe? I've tried to mask the small country sound I carried over after I left Wyoming.

"I don't know, somewhere over on the west coast." He pauses for a second. "You know you're only like two states away from me."

"I'm aware of that," I nod my head even though he can't see me. "But that doesn't solve the problem of the date."

"I told you I can get creative."

I throw the towel in the hamper beside my nightstand and lie back down on my bed. I yawn and cover my mouth, hoping he doesn't hear. "How does this creativity fit in?"

I hear a door open and close on his end of the phone. Is he home, or did he just walk out of the gym? This is the problem with long-distance dating. You don't know what the other person is doing, and you can't physically see them. I mean, I guess you can with video calling, but it's not the same.

"Well, I figure we grab food from the same burger place and watch a movie on Netflix while FaceTiming."

A burger does sound good. "Wait, I thought you said you eat healthy during the season."

"Normally, yes. A date, though...that calls for a cheat day. I'll just push harder at the gym tomorrow."

"We're doing it tonight?" My voice is high, and a jolt of panic rushes through me. My hair is a mess and my face is horrible.

"You don't have to get all dolled up," he says. "It's a simple movie night. If we were in the same place, I wouldn't be offended if you didn't dress up. I don't need all the glitz and glam. I'm actually a simple guy, despite what they portrayed in the media."

Does he know I looked him up? It's a natural assumption. I don't know anyone who goes on random dates without checking out the person's social media. You have to make sure you aren't dating a sociopath. "Okay," I drawl. "What burger place are we getting food from?"

"Whataburger, naturally." He's so confident in his answer, but...

"What is that?"

"Please tell me you're joking." He actually sounds pained that I have no clue what he's talking about. "They have some of the best burgers and amazing ketchup."

I wince, "Sorry, we don't have those here."

"Fine," he whines. "I guess any burger place will do.

Just know the next time you're in Texas, we are going to Whataburger. You'll be ruined for all future burger joints."

"I'll take your word for it." Staring at my ceiling, I mentally go through the list of everything I need to get done while I'm home. So much has to be crammed into such a short amount of time, and if I want to get any of it accomplished before this date, I need to get off the phone. "Hey, Bentley?"

"Yeah?"

"Can I talk to you later? Since I'm awake now, I need to get some errands done before tonight. Just text me what time you want to do this thing." It's been four days since I've talked to him, and while I think I could talk to him for hours, I can't. Adulting has to take precedence sometimes.

"Sure. I'll text you later." I'm about to hang up, but he speaks again. "I hope your day gets better and doesn't include any more water spills."

"Bye, Bentley," I smile and press the end icon.

There's no telling how this whole distance dating will go, and honestly, I'm a little worried he won't be faithful. But I have to do what I said. Take a chance and see what happens. At least he makes me laugh. Even if he calls at horrible hours of the morning.

What does one wear to a video date? I feel like if I dress in comfortable clothes… it's not enough. But, if I put on dressy clothes, I'm going to be uncomfortable. I know he said he didn't care if I was wearing pajamas, but that feels like I'll be copping out. This is why I stopped dating after Carter. Questioning everything from the wardrobe to the makeup and everything after that is exhausting.

A part of me wants to call and cancel. To text him and say I got food poisoning or something. There's no way he'd want to hang out on FaceTime if I'm "sick". Scratch that. He'd probably pry my address out of me and send someone with soup and crackers. He may give off this cocky persona, but I know there's a soft side to him. If I call off the date, I'll never find out and it'll eat at me until I can't take it anymore.

Screw it, I'm going to take his advice and be comfortable. Who the hell dresses up to hang out on their sofa all night? Not this gal. I rummage through the shelf in my closet until I find the perfect pair of yoga pants. Honestly, I should just call them comfy pants because they have never seen a yoga pose. Those paired with an oversize sweater should be good enough. If not, he can get over it.

I slide the sweater over my head, not bothering with a bra. One, I'm at home, there's no need to wear one. Two, he'll be looking at my face and this sweater is thick enough that if the phone drops, he won't see anything. I wasn't always this modest. Those nights going out with Lana, I was the life of the party. Heartbreak has a funny way of making you change. Time will tell if it's for the worse, or for the better. Bentley will either let me down, like every other person in my life aside from Lana. Or he'll be amazing. I'm really hoping for the latter. I don't think I can handle heartache twice in such a short amount of time.

My phone goes off as I'm shoving one of my legs into my yoga pants, and I almost trip as I scramble to the bed to grab it. I'm hoping it's Lana giving me a last-minute confidence boost, but the name on the screen is Bentley.

Bentley: Are you almost ready?

**Jolene: Yeah. Give me a few minutes. I'm
waiting for my food to get here.
Bentley: Okay. I'll call you in ten minutes.
Jolene: Sounds good.**

Crap. I hope the food gets here in time. I'm not a huge
fan of burgers, but that's what he wanted, so I searched
around for a decent-looking burger joint to order from. I
hope it's good. I added avocados to it hoping it will make it
taste better.

Rather than struggle to put my pants on while standing,
I lean back on the bed and pull them up. This is so much
easier, and it minimizes my chances of falling. All I need are
some cozy socks and to stalk to my door for the food.

Grabbing my charger from the nightstand, I hurry to the
living room. The delivery driver should be here in less than
five minutes. That gives me enough time to get Netflix, grab
something to drink, and pull out my favorite blanket. This
date will be comfortable all the way around. Even though
Bentley is getting creative, I'm not sure how I feel about
dating when I can't physically be around the person. The
whole point of watching a movie together is cuddling, and
I'm not about to cuddle with my phone. That's just weird.

A knock sounds at the door as I'm putting my bottle of
water on the coffee table. Thank God. There's only a few
minutes until Bentley is supposed to call me back. I open
the door without bothering to look through the peephole. A
young guy in a cap is standing in my doorway, a bag of food
in his outstretched hand. "Are you Jolene?"

"Yes," I say louder than needed. "Sorry, yes."

"Awesome," he sighs. "I went to the wrong floor and was
yelled at by some old dude. Anyway, here's your food."

"Thank you." I grab the cash I keep on the table beside my door and give him a tip. "Good luck on the rest of your deliveries. Hopefully, you don't get yelled at again."

"Thanks ma'am. Have a good night." He leaves as I shut the door, and the food smells delicious. I swear, if burgers smelled like this all the time, I'd probably eat them more often.

I hurry to the kitchen, grab a plate, and bring it to the living room. The ten minutes is almost up, and I'm setting my food out. I don't want the sound of a crinkling bag to ruin whatever plans Bentley has. In all of my rushing today to get my errands run, I didn't even ask him what movie we're watching. I guess I'm about to find out soon enough.

Grabbing my plate, I sit on the sofa, crossing my legs in front of me, and wait. My phone should be ringing any second now. A couple of minutes pass and he still hasn't called. Is he standing me up? He told me he'd call, and while I could call him, I'm not going to. He's the one that pushed for this date, and he should be the one that calls me.

I pick up my phone, checking to make sure it's not on silent. Nope, the little button is up, and there aren't any new messages from him. Something might have happened in the past fifteen minutes. He's just running late. A heads up would be nice. I didn't have any other plans tonight, but I don't want to stay up all night waiting for a call that might never come.

Another five minutes go by, and still nothing. My only company is my TV screen and Netflix showing me suggestions for what I should watch. Well, I guess I might as well start a new show and see if he ends up calling. Hopefully, my gut is wrong and the phone will ring soon.

FIFTEEN

Bentley

HOPEFULLY JOLENE IS ALL SET. I've got my bag from Whataburger and my TV queued up. This is definitely the most unique date I have ever had. The upside is there isn't any weird sending her home afterward, not that I would do that to her. I don't think, anyway. It's been years since a woman has gotten past date one. That's usually my limit. No further dates mean they don't walk out on me later. It's also the reason I usually dismiss the women I'm with. No attachments. Jolene is different, though. Something about her calls to me.

I grab my phone off the end table and hover above her name, but my screen flashes with an incoming call. Derrick's name pops up, and he has the worst timing ever. I haven't heard from him in weeks, and this is the time he calls. I could always reject it and act like I didn't hear the phone. He's persistent, though. He has been since the day I met him and he wanted me to help him get ready for basketball tryouts at Hilltown University. He badgered every senior on the team until I finally agreed. Other than that short amount of time he let an old flame get in his head, he was dedicated.

The urge to press the red button is strong, but he'll just keep calling until I answer. He knows I'm usually free, and wouldn't think I might have plans. Sighing, I press the button to accept the call. "Hey, Derrick."

"Hey, man. How are things?" There's no pause for me to answer before he's charging into the next question. "Dude, we're struggling as a team. I have no idea what to do. It's like when you left, the rest of the team just kind of gave up. It's hurting our chances for playoffs."

I pull the phone away from my ear and check the time. Shit, it's a few minutes past the time I was supposed to call Jolene. "Look D, now isn't really—"

He cuts me off. "Please, Bentley. We have a game tomorrow and the guys are acting like we've already lost. We need your help."

"I'm not sure what you expect me to do. It's not like I can come play for y'all."

"I know that." He sounds frustrated. I know playing for Hilltown is one of his greatest accomplishments, and he wants the team to get another winning title. "Is there any way you can come talk to the team? Anything for these guys to get their heads out of their asses."

"You sound desperate," I hear in the background. It must be his roommate. "Maybe you should lead with a question instead of demanding time from him. He's busy, too."

I can't remember the guy's name, but I like the way he thinks. The few times I was around him, he seemed to have his head on straight. Even when he got with that party girl. Well, former party girl. She's mellowed out a lot since they got together. Now if only Derrick would take some of those cues.

"Shut up, Travis. You stick to your books and let us talk ball." As dedicated as Derrick is to the game, he lets it consume him. If I don't put an end to this, he'll keep me on the phone all night.

"Derrick, this really isn't a good time. I'm late for a date. Text me with the info about your game. If I'm out of practice in time, I'll swing by the university and talk to the guys." Hopefully that's enough to placate him.

"Oh shit, I'm sorry." He pauses for a second. "I'll text that to you in just a few. Have fun on your date. I hope she's hot." I hear something smack him, and he says, "Ow."

"That's not funny, Derrick." His girlfriend's voice is really loud, and I know she must be right there. "You better not be thinking about hot girls."

They will be at this for a while. "Bye, Derrick," I yell louder than necessary and hang up the phone. Talking to him can be draining at times. He's almost never alone, and the conversations are always competing.

I look at the time and groan. I'm almost twenty minutes late for my date. I press Jolene's number and listen to the ring. Please pick up. Pick up. Pick up. Pick up. The phone rings so long, I think it's going to rollover to voicemail. Luckily, Jolene has mercy on me. "Hello?"

Damn, not good. Her voice is clipped. "Sorry, I'm late. One of my old teammates called and wouldn't shut up."

"It's fine." Those two words are not in fact fine. I've heard my mom and sister mutter them on more than one occasion. They weren't happy any of those times.

"Really, Jolene." I hope she can hear the sincerity in my voice. "I'm sorry. Please tell me you at least already ate your food. There's no use letting it get cold."

"I'm not a dumbass," she scoffs. "But yes, I already ate. Do you still want to try this whole date thing?"

"Yeah. Maybe we can talk instead. It's getting kind of late for a movie." I wait for a rebuttal, but it doesn't come. "Unless, you're ready to go to bed. In that case, you could take me with you."

"Men," she grumbles. "I swear that's all you think about."

"Not true," I grin. "I also think about food, working out, basketball..."

"So, it's in the top five." She laughs, and I think I've gotten her in a better mood. "I thought you were going to FaceTime me?"

I don't respond. Instead, I press the icon for FaceTime and she switches over to video. Her hair is up in a messy ponytail thing and she looks like she's ready for bed. "You just couldn't go without looking at this handsome face, could you?"

She rolls her eyes, but the corner of her mouth quirks up. "Shut up. I'm just making sure we're sticking to our date agreement. You're the one who pushed for us to have the date over the phone."

"That's because I know it won't happen otherwise. At least, not until we're in the same town again." I lean into the corner of my couch. "And I'm not sure when that will happen. I need to look on my schedule."

"Why would you have to look at your schedule?"

Shit, Lana never told her she gave me her schedule. Do I tell her and risk pissing her off, or do I act like its pure coincidence? "Um, because that has my out-of-town dates on it?"

"You framed that as a question." She stands up and I see the kitchen cabinets behind her. They are an off-white color and look old. Does she live in an older unit? Maybe it's one of those that has the country feel to it like a lot of the houses here in Texas. I swear after that couple down in Waco got that decorating show, people have been redecorating their homes to match their style.

Jolene raises an eyebrow and I know she's still waiting on a response. Damn it, I'm going to have to tell her. "So, you know how you refused to go out on a date with me after that first flight?"

"Yes, but I don't see what that has to do with anything."

Please don't be pissed, is all I chant to myself before I tell her the next part. "Well, I ran into Lana at the hotel, and she kinda, sorta gave me your flight schedule so I could book my flights to correspond with yours."

"She did WHAT?" Her voice is definitely on the screeching side, and I think I may have just fucked up. "I can't believe the nerve of her. No wonder she's been pushing so hard for us to date. And you," she looks me square in the eyes through the screen. "You went along with it? You didn't think it was overstepping any boundaries?"

"I wanted to go on a date with you," I shrug my shoulders, indifferent. "And she was willing to make that happen. The more chances you had to be around me, the more chances I had of you saying yes."

Her face is turning red, and I don't know if it's from anger or something else. "You realize that's creepy, right? That would be the equivalent of one of your little fans following you home and waiting outside your house."

"Believe it or not, that's happened before."

"So, you think it's okay for you to do it?" Yep, anger is the reason she's turning colors. But she sits back down and takes a deep breath, trying to calm herself down.

"Would you have gone on a date with me otherwise?"

She taps her finger against her chin, thinking, and quiet for way too long. "I don't know. I kind of wrote you off after that first meeting. You're way too sure of yourself and not really my type."

"And what is your type? Someone who has their shit together? Or someone who only uses you for what they want and discards you when they're done? Because I sometimes fall into both categories, and I'm willing to see where this goes."

Her head rears back as if I have slapped her. I guess I hit a little too close to home. "If you are the second type, I don't know that this is worth pursuing."

I won't apologize for who I've been. Getting romantically involved with someone when they may leave is terrifying and not necessarily something I want to go through. "I said sometimes. And just so you know, I haven't been with or even tried to see anyone else since that first flight." That's something I didn't want to admit, but if it will ease her worries, so be it. "You want to know why I haven't seen anyone?" She shakes her head no even though her eyes are pleading for the answer. "Because I saw the way you reacted to that guy, and how much he must have hurt you. You intrigue me, and I know that the only way I'd have a shot is if I didn't keep up my player ways."

Her lips are pressed firmly together and I want her to tell me what she's thinking. I'm not one to play games, and she'll accept me or she won't. This is not at all how I envisioned our first personal date going. It was supposed to be happy and watching a movie. Not getting into the nitty gritty bullshit that is going to run her off. I probably could have censored my answers better, but I also don't want to give her a false sense of who I am.

Finally, she speaks. "I'm not sure what to say. You're

definitely not the type I would normally date. You have heartbreak written all over you. But I guess if you're willing to give this thing a shot, then I am, too." Her eyes shift to the side, uncertain if this is something she really wants to do.

"Only if you're certain," I say. "I don't want to get into this thing and then you back out because you're scared. That's not fair to either of us."

She takes a deep breath then releases it. "I'm sure." She nods to drive the point home and I do a mental fist in the air. Damn, I've never had to work this hard to get someone's attention. "What do we do now?"

"Talk. That's what most people do on the phone." Honestly, this is the longest I've ever been on the phone with someone other than my mom or sister. They'll talk my ear off for hours. "What if we did this crazy thing called getting to know each other?"

"Okay," she drawls. "What's your family like?"

Damn, that's not where I expected this to go. Most women I've seen have wanted to know about my career and how I got signed right out of college. "It's just me, my mom, and sister. My mom worked a lot when we were growing up to put food on the table, so Gabby and I pretty much raised ourselves. We're all pretty close to each other. Mom likes to meddle in my business, so I don't tell her as much as she'd like. She only does it because she cares, though. My sister is the closest thing to a best friend I've ever had, and I don't know what I would do without her."

"What about your dad?"

Now it's my turn to take a deep breath. He's a sore subject, but if I'm going to give this thing with her an actual shot..."He's been out of the picture since I was six. One minute we were this small happy family, and the next he was gone. Just walked out and never came back."

"Wow. I'm so sorry." There's sadness in her eyes, but it's not just for me and my family.

"It is what it is. I spent years trying to figure out what I did wrong. How I could have made him stay, but in the end, I realized he's a douche for walking out and leaving us wondering." Time to change the subject. I don't want to think about my dad. "What about your family?" They have to be better than mine.

"I don't know. I haven't talked to them in years."

Or maybe not. "Why?"

"They didn't support my dream of traveling the world. They wanted me to go to college and find a real job. I didn't want to do that. When I decided to be a flight attendant, they told me I could come back home when I decided to grow up and be an adult. That was almost five years ago."

"That's harsh. I guess we both have assholes in our families."

"Yep. I won't say I don't miss them, but they only supported me when I fell in line with what they wanted. And that's just not something I want to deal with. I met Lana when I was training to be a flight attendant, and she's been my family since then."

"I'm happy you have that. Other than my actual family, my team from college is like my family. We did everything together. Right now, they are struggling, so I'm going to give them a pep talk tomorrow. That's the reason I was late calling. My former teammate, Derrick, called me freaking out about their playoff chances."

"That's cool they still come to you for advice. How long have you been playing basketball?"

I glance around my empty walls, wishing I would have brought some of my awards with me just so I could show her. That's something that needs to be rectified soon.

Maybe I'll have Gabby come decorate for me, but with not so much girly shit. I want this to look like an actual home if Jolene ever comes to Austin. "Since I was a kid. Mom and Gabby didn't want me to get mixed up in any sketchy shit, so they put me in a basketball program at the civic center. I never had any aspirations to play until then. After that, I did everything I could to become better. I started watching old college and NBA games to study the sport. I practiced every day. Even when it was raining until Mom would make me come into the garage so I wouldn't track water throughout the house."

A smile graces her lips and I know she's impressed. That's not why I told her, though. It was my life. It is my life. "That's some serious dedication."

"I wanted to be the best," I grin. "It finally paid off."

"That it did," she yawns. "Sorry, I didn't mean to do that. It happens when I sit still for too long."

"Go get some sleep." I glance at the clock, realizing a couple of hours have passed by. I guess time flies when you're arguing then learning about each other.

"No, really, I'm fine," she says through another yawn.

"Clearly." I stand up and walk toward my bedroom. "We can always continue the conversation in bed."

"I'm not having phone or video sex with you on our second date." She scrunches up her nose, and it's adorable.

"Who has their mind in the gutter now?" I laugh and continue up the stairs. "I only meant that I'll stay on until one of us falls asleep."

"That's weird." But she stands and walks a scant distance until I see her head hit a fluffy white pillow. "I haven't done this since I was a kid talking to my friends."

"I've never done this. At least, not that I can remember."

"Too many drunken nights?" I'm not sure if I should be offended or not.

"For your information, I rarely drink."

"You were drinking at the bar the other night."

"Yeah, because I was frustrated and talking shop with one of my teammates. I don't need alcohol to have a good time."

"That's good to know." Her voice is soft and slow. Her eyes are shut, and I know this conversation is over.

"Goodnight, Jolene."

A soft murmur is her response, and I hit the end button. The "date" started off rocky, and I wasn't sure it was going to pan out. But I'm relieved we turned it around. Maybe this whole dating thing won't be a terrible idea. The first time I've actually dated someone since I was in high school. My first instinct is to text Gabby, or Jordan, and tell them all about it, like some over-excited teenage girl. But I refrain. If I text Gabby, she'll be pissed. Or, she'll call and I'll be on the phone forever. It's already late and I don't need that kind of talk right now. I'll call her tomorrow while I'm on the way to Hilltown U. That provides me with a time limit and I'll be able to cut her off.

I take off my pants and slide under the covers of my bed. It'd be a lot better if I had a certain someone beside me, but we'll get to that. For now, I need to focus on one thing at a time, and right now...that's sleep.

SIXTEEN

Jolene

"So, how are things going with Bentley?" Lana asks me as we board the plane. "Good, I'm assuming."

I stow my bag and suitcase in a compartment and grab the cleaning supplies. "I'm sure the attendants on the previous flight already did this, but I feel the need to do something to keep myself occupied. "Things are going really well. We've had a couple of phone dates."

"How exactly does that work?" She's fixing her hair, getting it out of her face, and walking down the aisle instead of helping me clean anything. "I mean, seriously, what can you do over the phone? Unless...you're doing something naughty." She wiggles her eyebrows at me and I want to smack her.

Bentley has joked with me about it, but I always change the subject. It's not that I don't want to be physical with him. He's hot as hell, and I have a feeling he knows how to satisfy women. I just...I'm not ready to hop into bed with him. Even though I know him better than I did before, I still don't know if I can trust him. "You're just as bad as the dudes who only think about jumping into the sack."

"I happen to think I have an amazing sex life. I don't have to love the guy...he just needs to pique my interest." She finally grabs some cleaning products and wipes down the armrests on the other aisle. "When will you see him again?"

"I feel like you should know the answer to that since you gave him my schedule." I wasn't going to tell her I know what she did, but the opportunity presented itself.

She stills. "I'm not sure what you mean?"

"I'm not mad." Well, I was for about two seconds, but it's not a horrible thing. I do like the guy. "He let it slip during our first phone date."

"Whew," she sighs. "I was worried you would hate me. But you definitely needed that extra push. You sure as hell weren't going to do it yourself."

"Thanks. I think." We finish our cleaning and straighten up the refreshments. Now, we wait until it's time to welcome our new passengers. "Anyway, we have a layover in Austin, and I'm planning to see him before the flight that he's on. We probably won't do much since there isn't much time."

"I know some things you can do that don't take too long," she winks.

"Lana, if it isn't going to take very long, I'm not sure I'd want him in my bed."

"You have a point there." The pilot comes over the intercom, letting us know passengers are about to board. "Well, let's get this show on the road. You have a hottie to see."

Even though we've talked frequently for over a week, this is the first time I'll see him since we were in Chicago.

Nerves eat away at me, and I hope he still wants to see me. Why is dating so hard? Better yet, how are we going to greet each other? A hug and a kiss seem too forward, but I want to feel the press of his lips against mine. I mean, it's not like we're total strangers. We've eaten dinner together over multiple phone calls. We've even cooked together.

The first passenger walks onto the plane and shakes me out of my thoughts. I can worry about that when we get closer to Austin. For now, I have a job to do, even if I'm beginning to wish I had a steadier job just so I could see Bentley in person more often. As crazy as it sounds, I'm growing fond of him.

The plane touches down and the wait for the passengers to get off is torture. On one hand, I want them to hurry so I can see Bentley. On the other hand...I want them to take forever because I don't know what to expect. Will he be waiting for me inside the airport, or will I have to find him?

With all the passengers gone, and the cleaning done, it's time to meet up with Bentley. I grab my suitcase and bag while checking my phone. There aren't any texts from him, and I'm worried he forgot about me.

Lana throws her arm around me as we make our way through the airport. "Are you ready to see your man?"

"I'm not sure I'd call him my man just yet. We're still getting to know each other." There's a bathroom up ahead and I steer us in that direction to change. "Besides, I haven't heard from him yet. Who knows if he's even coming?"

"I'm sure he'll have something amazing planned for you."

"Are the two of you orchestrating things behind my

back again?" I rush into the stall and start peeling off my clothes. "Now that we're dating, you don't have to do that anymore."

"Nope. I have no clue what he has planned for you." She reaches her hand over the door for my uniform so I can change into my normal clothes. "I haven't talked to him since I sent him your schedule. Everything else has been all him."

"That's good to know," I murmur, pulling my shirt over my head. "What am I going to do if he doesn't show up?"

"You'll call me, and we'll go grab lunch somewhere close by."

I pull up my jeans and slide my feet into the Vans I keep in my carryon. I pull the door open and wave my arms as if I'm on display. "How do I look?"

Lana nods her head and grins. "Amazing. Like the girl next door, but not trying too hard. You just need one more thing." She reaches above me and pulls the hair tie out of my hair. My hair falls down my back. "There, that's better. You're ready to go now."

We walk out of the bathroom and toward the entrance. A man stands by the front door with a sign that says Jolene. "What are the chances there's another Jolene coming off a flight right now?"

She shrugs, "I mean there's a possibility, but I'm going to say it's slim. We should go see if it's for you."

The guy with the sign is looking around the airport. Obviously, whoever hired him didn't give him a description of the person they are picking up. "I don't know if I should go up to this guy." That could be someone else's ride, and I'd feel terrible if I took it by mistake.

"No worries," Lana chirps. She rushes to the man in question, barely stopping before barreling him over. "Sir, can I ask who sent you to pick up Jolene?" She points to the sign as if he doesn't remember.

He takes a step back from her, uncomfortable with how much she's in his personal space. "Yes, I'm the driver on standby for the Austin Rattlers. Bentley sent me to pick her up."

Whirling around, Lana throws her hands on her hips and gives me a satisfied smirk. "I told you he wasn't here for another Jolene."

I hate admitting she's right, and I refuse to give her that victory. A pang of sadness hits me in my gut. He couldn't even come get me himself? He had to send the driver for his team to do it for him. "Okay, so I guess I'm going with this mystery man and hoping he takes me to Bentley."

Lana puts an arm around my shoulder, almost having to stand on her toes. "Don't worry. I'm sure there's an excellent reason for sending a driver. If anything looks sketchy, send me your location on your phone and I'll come in for the rescue." Her whisper is just loud enough to be heard by the driver, and he raises an eyebrow.

"I'll be fine," I force a smile. "I'll see you before the next flight out. Meet you at the gate?"

"Yep," she squeezes me one more time. "Have fun and try not to be too mad at him for not picking you up himself."

"Are you ready, Ms. Jolene?" He holds his hand out for my suitcase. Wow. He called me "Ms." I don't think anyone has ever called me that in my life. It must be a Southern thing, but it makes me feel old.

"Sure," I pass the rolling suitcase over to him. "Mr...." I let my voice trail off, waiting for him to supply his name.

"You can call me Sam." We stroll out of the airport as if we aren't on any kind of schedule. I only have so many hours before I have to be back at the airport. There isn't time to dawdle. Not if I want to spend any sort of valuable time with Bentley.

"Where is Bentley?" Maybe Sam can give me a clue.

"I can't tell you that."

"Why?" He leads me to a sleek black car and opens the door for me. I lean against the door, waiting for him to answer me.

"He said it's a surprise." Okay. I guess that's the only answer I'm going to get. I slide into the backseat and he closes the door. After stopping for a second behind the car, he gets behind the wheel. "It's nothing bad, I promise."

"If you say so." I put on my seatbelt as Sam pulls into traffic. Tall buildings loom above us, and I'm pretty sure we're heading into downtown. I spot the capitol building, and I would love to tour it one day. Next time I'm in Austin, I'll plan on stopping by. I'll drag Lana along with me even though she hates that sort of thing.

A few minutes go by and we pull up to a rectangular building that is nowhere near as tall as the ones surrounding it. Before I can even reach for the handle Sam is at my door, pulling it open. "What is this place?"

"You'll see." He gestures for me to follow him.

"What about my suitcase?"

"It'll be here. I'm your driver for the rest of the day." Is Bentley really that important to have his own personal driver?

I shove my hands in my pockets as he leads us into the building. This whole thing is weird. As we walk through the hallway, I hear bouncing coming from somewhere ahead of us. Surely Bentley doesn't have a game today. This place isn't exactly where I'd picture a professional team playing. We enter a gym, and a group of guys is playing basketball. They seem like giants compared to me. My eyes search the court until I find him. He's hard to see with most of the guys towering over him. He's tall, but he's not that tall.

Sam points toward the bleachers, "You can sit up there. They'll be done soon."

I do as he says and notice a group of younger guys sitting at the opposite end. They are focused on the team bouncing the ball on the court. Bentley doesn't notice my arrival, of course. His head is in the game, or maybe practice.

Sports have never really been my thing. I would catch a few minutes of a game if I was at a bar with Lana, but other than that, I've never sought out a game to watch. I can see why people gravitate toward basketball, though. It's fast-paced, and my head swivels from one side to the other trying to figure out what they are doing. Someone blows a whistle. The guys on the court split up into two groups and head toward the side of the court. They are passing water bottles around, and the thought of sharing a bottle with someone sends a shiver down my spine. Their lips never touch it. But I didn't even share with my siblings growing up. I don't want their germs mingling with my germs, thank you very much.

Less than a minute passes and they are back on the court. Something on the wall catches my eye, and it's the scoreboard. There are literally seconds left in the game. I wish I had gotten here sooner to see Bentley play more. He obviously wanted to share this moment with me. Wanted me to see this part of his life and how passionate he is about it.

The buzzer sounds, and the players split up again. The group Bentley is with give each other high fives and are talking smack to the other team. His eyes lift up and search the bleachers and he smiles wide when he sees me. He holds a finger up, letting me know he'll come over in a moment. The man with the whistle waves his hand toward the young men sitting on the bleachers and they rush the court. They are wide-eyed and murmuring to each other. This must be their first time seeing them, too.

Bentley pulls one of the guys away from the group and stalks toward me. He looks hot, and not because he just finished playing. His arm muscles are on full display thanks to the sleeveless shirt he's wearing. I'm almost certain the temperature in here went up ten degrees. I lift my hand to fan myself, but force it back down. It's too early for him to know that he has this effect on me. Hell, it's too early for me to even be feeling this way toward him. Shit. This man is already working his way into my emotions and we've only been on one proper date.

SEVENTEEN

Bentley

My sole focus is on her. It has been since I caught her walking into the gym. Jordan and Derrick should be able to handle things for a minute. They get to see their girls every day. This is the first time I've seen Jolene in almost two weeks.

As much as I want to run to her and spin her around like in one of those stupid romantic movies, I don't. I can't have her knowing she's the one person I've been thinking of more and more lately. At least, not yet. "You made it."

"Yeah," she smiles and takes in the group of basketball players on the court. "Is this some sort of game, or something? I've never been to any kind of sports game."

What? That seems crazy to me, but not everyone is into sports the way I am. "Not really." I wave my hand to the guys. "It's a mini practice, but also a teaching opportunity."

"Do you do things like this often?"

"Sometimes. But it's usually with youth sports programs, not college kids that have lost their mojo." I grab her hand and bring her into a hug. She doesn't shy away from my sweaty body and I'm relieved. Most of the women I've dated in the past are grossed out by sweat. They didn't want to touch me until I cleaned up. The fact that Jolene has zero qualms about it has to mean something, right? If anything, it shows that she's willing to accept me, even when I'm disgusting.

"I'm guessing these are the guys from your university. The ones you gave a pep talk to?" Her breath is soft against my neck and the guys on the court are the last thing I'm thinking about.

I slowly pull away to keep myself in check. "Uh yeah, that would be them. I wish you could see more of our practice, though."

"Sorry," she winces. "I had to change after we landed, and I thought Lana was going to interrogate your driver for a minute." She scrunches her nose, and it's adorable. "By the way, why do we have a driver?"

"Oh, Derrick," I point to him standing next to Jordan, "picked me up on the way here. He wanted pointers and to see what I thought about the rest of the season. I didn't want to have to drive back to my house and force you to deal with his constant questions. Sam usually only drives for the important people on the team, but he agreed to drive us around, so I'd have more time with you. And because I'm his favorite player on the team."

He's standing nearby and rolls his eyes at the last comment. "You're all a pain in my ass." He shakes his head and moves closer to the team. "Don't forget, you'll need to come over for a photo before we leave. The owners aren't going to miss a good PR moment."

Crap, I forgot about that. We probably should have

done that before we started. "Let me go wrangle these guys together so we can get out of here."

"Sounds good. I'll just be right over there," she points to the bleachers. She probably wants to sit after being on her feet for who knows how long. I know I would if I had to stand nonstop during a flight. I don't think I've ever seen her sit while she's working.

"I'll make it quick." Jogging over to the guys, I see Ross shake his head, and I shoot him a glare to not open his mouth.

He obviously doesn't heed my warning, or thinks I'm playing around. He walks over to me and grins. "I see she's gotten under your skin. I thought y'all were dating for fun." He raises an eyebrow in question.

"We are. But it's difficult to date someone when you live in different states." I don't know why I'm so defensive. Maybe it's because he's acknowledging things I'm not ready to accept. I mean, we aren't completely serious, even though we aren't seeing other people. But it's not like we're proclaiming our undying love for each other. Hell, we haven't even been intimate yet.

"All I'm saying," Ross continues, "Is that nobody else brings their girl to practice unless they are married, or ready to take things to the next level."

"Stop giving Bentley a hard time," Jordan says from behind me. "He'll realize for himself, eventually."

Great, now they are both on my case. "Whatever. Let's get this over with so I can take Jolene on a date before she has to fly off again." I immediately wish I would have picked a better phrase. Let's be real, that's how this is going to end. She'll constantly be flying off to her next adventure and I'll be the one waiting for the next phone call, or visit, wondering if she's going to leave forever.

I shake the thought from my mind. "All right guys, let's get this show on the road. I've got things to do." A series of whistles sounds around me, and I glance up at Jolene. Her cheeks are bright pink, and she knows she's the reason for the sudden noise. "Shut up and let's do this thing."

Derrick stands next to me with a knowing smile. "Don't say a word," I warn. He still looks up to me and lifts his hands in surrender.

The rest of the guys gather around us with Coach standing on the end. Normally, he'd be in the middle with all the players surrounding him, but he doesn't like being the center of attention. Sam grabs his phone out of his back pocket and holds it in front of him. "Okay guys, smile big. I'm going to take a few shots and they can figure out which one they want to use."

We do as we're told and step away from each other as soon as Sam puts his phone down. Derrick claps me on the shoulder, "Good luck on your date. If you need any help in the future, all you have to do is call."

"Yeah, okay," I snort. "If you think I'm taking dating advice from you, you're nuts. How long did it take for you to get things right with Darcy?"

"We aren't talking about me right now," he waves the comment away. "You date and go through women like you change your underwear. They never last long with you, and I know that's how you prefer it." I open my mouth to interrupt, but he plows ahead. "I see how you've been looking at her, and how she was watching you. She's not like the others. Not by a long shot. She's one of those you take home to your parents and make a real go of it. It's scary, but don't let that fear get in the way of something good."

He hit the nail on the head without realizing it. I've never told him any of the fears I have over people leaving.

But I guess he knows how to spot it considering the lengths his roommate went through to get the girl he wants. "I think you're spending too much time with Darcy. She's turning you into someone who thinks logically."

"Blame her if you want, but you know I'm right."

I'll never admit that. "Then you need to do the same thing with the team. They need a leader. Someone who will tell them, and guide them through, what they need to do. You may be one of the youngest on the team, but you have what it takes. Getting them here today was the first step. Finish taking that role by leading them toward a championship." Yes, I feel like a hypocrite even as the words come out of my mouth. But the advice can be applied with both situations. The only way we'll both get what we want is if we take a leap. It's time for me to take mine. "Let me know if you want to get together to shoot around."

"Will do," he grins. As annoying as Derrick can be, he's the only genuine friend I have outside of the team. "And remember what I said."

"Yep." I head toward the sideline and grab my open gym bag. I pull out my sweats and hoodie, slipping them on before walking to Jolene. "You ready to get out of here?"

"Sure." Her smile brightens up her face, and I know that she's happy to be here. She doesn't say anything about the fact I haven't showered and don't plan to. It would take away time from her. She wraps an arm around my waist and points toward the door, "Show me what Austin has to offer."

"This wasn't what I was expecting." She slides out of the backseat after me, and stares at the fast-food restaurant in front of us. Sam already told me he's going to go down the street for tacos and will be back before we're done. He's burned out on this place, and I'm not sure how that's possible.

It's definitely not the most romantic date, but I warned her. "You are about to have your taste buds changed forever." She side-eyes me and I chuckle. "I told you the first thing we would do when you had a few hours in Texas was get Whataburger." I stretch out my arms in front of me as if I'm displaying a prize on a TV game show. "I make good on my promises."

"I guess we're about to see if it's as good as you say it is." I take hold of her hand and we make our way to the automatic doors. As soon as it slides open, Jolene takes a big sniff. "It smells amazing. Like camp cookouts and grills."

I mentally high five myself. She could have been disgusted when we showed up here, but she's taking it all in stride. I have a feeling Mom and Gabby will love her. Well, when the time comes for her to meet them. Derrick's words from the gym come back to me. That's not today, though.

She studies the menu as we wait in line. "Which is better? Onion rings or fries?"

"You really can't go wrong. Either way, make sure you get the spicy ketchup. It's a game changer."

We place our order and find a table in the corner. I shouldn't get too much attention here since we're in my old neighborhood. Even though I've gone pro, they still treat me the same. It's kind of jarring to the way other people act around me, but it's a small way of keeping me humble. Jolene sits down on the bench beside me and bumps her shoulder into mine. "Doesn't eating here go against all the healthy eating practices you set for yourself during the season?"

Shrugging my shoulders, I lift my arm and rest it on

her shoulder before pulling her closer to me. Having her here with me feels natural and right. "Yeah, but I'm willing to have cheat days if it means being with you." Ugh, I sound so cheesy. Why does she throw me off my game?

"Aw, I'm worthy of a cheat day." It's weird seeing her all cuddly and leaning into me. It's a far cry from how she was when we first met. Maybe she's decided to let go and take a leap herself.

I brush my fingertips along her arm and she shivers. "You are worth so much more." And it's true. I've never put this much effort into dating anyone, much less someone that lives in another state.

"You have no idea how refreshing it is to hear that." Sadness fills her voice, and I have a feeling it has to deal with more than just her parents shunning her decisions. Now isn't the time to dig around for the cause. I have my suspicions but we're in public and I don't want to make her uncomfortable.

One of the employees, Brandy, shows up with our tray of food and sets it down on the table. She reaches for the number they gave us when we ordered, but I slide it to the wall. "Is there any way I can keep this one?"

She shakes her head. "You've been here enough times to know I can't do that."

"Come on," I argue. "You won't miss one little number, Brandy. I'll even pay you for it."

"Bentley, you know I--"

I cut her off before she can say that negative four-letter word. "This is Jolene's first time inside a Whataburger. She needs a memento to remind her how amazing it is when she's back at home."

Jolene has been watching us go back and forth until she

hears her name. "Oh no, it's fine. I can grab a picture by the sign, or something."

I stare at Brandy, willing her not to make a big deal out of this. I mean, it's one stupid plastic tent. We were friends, sort of, back in high school. Why is she making this such a big deal? Brandy glances over at Jolene, and I'm not sure what she sees on her face, but she relents. "You can keep it, but I'm telling your mom you're being a pain"

I sag in relief, but worry over what she's going to say to Mom is going to plague me. I haven't mentioned Jolene to her yet. Even though I've talked to her a few times since Jolene and I started dating. I don't want to get her hopes up. "Thank you," I call to Brandy's retreating back.

"You didn't have to do that," Jolene nudges me in the ribs with her elbow.

"What are you talking about? Everyone needs a souvenir from their first time here." I separate our food and unwrap her burger for her. She serves and takes care of people all day. I wonder if she's ever had anyone cater to her. "I can't wait to see what you think."

She picks up the burger and eyes it before looking at me. "I hope this is as good as you say. I don't even like burgers in general."

I pull my hand to my chest. "You wound me. How can you not like burgers?"

"I don't know," she shrugs. "They're fine, I just never really cared for them." She takes a bite and groans. "This is actually really good," she says while covering her mouth full of food. "I think it's the avocado."

In my opinion it's sacrilege to put that on a burger, but if she likes it that way, who am I to argue. "I told you. Just wait until you dip an onion ring into the ketchup. It's so popular they sell it in certain grocery stores."

"Are you serious?"

"Yep. If you end up liking it, I'll ship you some."

An alarm on a phone goes off, and she rummages around her bag. "Crap. We'll have to wrap this up pretty quickly. I need to head to the airport soon."

"You set an alarm to remind you?"

"Well, yeah," she replies, sheepish. "I didn't know what we would be doing. And I didn't want to get so lost in the moment that I lost track of time and missed my flight."

She's responsible, and it's one of the things I admire about her. She understands dedication and doesn't give in to her whims. No matter how much I wish she would. "Well, let's hurry up and finish eating. I'll text Sam and let him know we're almost ready." Having to cut this short isn't what I had in mind, but I understand. She has a job, like I do, and she takes it seriously.

Sam pulls up to the drop off area of the airport and I'm not ready for the day to end. Not ready for her to get on a plane and leave me. Our driver exits the car to get her luggage from the trunk. "Do you want me to walk you in?" We're still in the bubble of the backseat, and it'll burst the second Jolene reaches for the door.

"No," she shakes her head. "There's a separate entrance for us to enter, and they don't let others come through."

"Oh," I nod. "I have a flight with you in a couple of days. We can grab dinner after that. Maybe have an overnight visit..." I let the sentence trail off to see what she does with information. I'm not pushing to have sex, yet. She's skittish at the best of times anytime I broach the subject. If it were up to me, I'd take her in the backseat now.

I'm trying to be a gentleman and give her what she deserves. Not a rushed moment of passion that she may regret later.

"We can definitely get together." She doesn't acknowledge the last sentence, but she also seems hesitant to leave the car. The weight of ending our date must be heavy for her. "I should probably go."

She reaches for the door, and my stomach sinks. Fuck being a gentleman. I'm not letting her leave this car without giving her something to remember until the next time we see each other.

Before she can touch the handle, I pull her toward me and fuse my mouth to hers. She stiffens in surprise, then melts into my arms. Her tongue slides across the seam of my lips, and I grant her entry. More than willing to let her lead the kiss. Let her decide how much she wants to give. Our tongues tangle together and she wraps her arms around my neck, bringing her even closer. If I pull her onto my lap, she'd see just how much more I want.

My hand glides up her back before sliding into her hair. I grasp the locks in my fist and pull her head back a fraction of an inch, exposing her long, slender neck. Breaking the kiss, my mouth trails down her skin and her barely audible gasps send blood straight to my cock. As torturous as this is for me, I can only imagine what it's doing to her. I want nothing more than to slide my other hand into her jeans to see how much I'm affecting her.

I slowly work my way back to her lips, and her phone rings. It's loud in the silence of the backseat. She pulls away from me and I let my hands fall to my lap, adjusting my sweats. "That's probably Lana wondering where I am." Her voice is ragged and her lips are plump. There's no way to deny my mouth hasn't been on hers. Thank god Sam didn't come back into the car.

"Saved by the phone once again," I grin. Lifting a hand, I smooth out her hair, trying to make her look presentable.

"Yeah. She must have a weird sixth sense." Her eyes linger on my lips before she shakes her head. "I better go before she sends out the calvary."

"That's a good idea. She terrifies me."

"I'll see you on the next flight?" she asks, as if I would change my flight schedules now.

"Absolutely. Let me know when you get to wherever you're going."

She nods her agreement. "Thank you for today, Bentley. I'll call you later." With that, she's out of the car. She pauses long enough to get her luggage from Sam, then she's walking into the airport.

Sam slides into the driver's seat. "You're welcome."

"You're such an asshole," I mumble. I'm grateful he gave me a few moments with her, but I think I miss her more now. "Any chance you can take me home?"

"Of course." He glances in the review mirror, "What kind of jackass would I be if I made you call an Uber to get you home after that."

"You saw?" I hope Jolene doesn't realize that. She'll be mortified.

"The tint is dark, but not that dark."

"Whatever," I roll my eyes. "Let's get out of here."

We've only been on two physical dates, but she's wormed her way into my thoughts. There's no way I will be able to sleep tonight. I pull my phone off the seat and open up my text messages.

Bentley: You up for coming over and playing video games.

Derrick: Yep. Be there in two hours. Is it cool if Darcy comes?
Bentley: I assume that means Cam & Travis will be coming, too…
Derrick: Probably.
Bentley: Come on then.

They are the distraction I need to get my head out of the gutter. Or at least I hope so. They better not come at me with relationship advice.

EIGHTEEN

Jolene

I CAN'T STOP THINKING about that first kiss, or the ones we've shared since. Over the past few weeks, I swear it looks like I've gotten lip injections from how swollen they are. We're like teenagers making out as much as we can when we see each other. It's not uncalled for since we rarely see each other. Video calls over the phone don't count and are nowhere near enough. Now, more than ever, I wish I had a job that didn't require me to be gone so much. If that was the case, though, I wouldn't have met him. I don't think we would have ever crossed paths. I just wish I had more time that I could see him.

My relationship with Bentley feels like it did when I was with Carter, but different. All the giddy newness is there, but it feels like more. Like things could really progress with us and that thought terrifies me. It's probably not right that I'm comparing the two, but it's hard. I thought I had more with Carter, except I didn't. I wasn't the one meant for him. Fear pulses through my veins, and I need to tamp that down. They aren't the same.

Lana pulls me aside before passengers leave the plane. "Are you going out with Bentley tonight?"

The man in question is sitting in the middle of the center aisle. It warms my heart that even though he has the ability to fly first class, he doesn't. He chooses to fly coach so he can see me. "Yeah. We have a reservation for dinner."

She waggles her eyebrows at me. "Are you going to take it to the next level? I mean, you don't even have to go to a hotel tonight because we're home. You can just take him straight to your own bed."

"Oh my God, Lana." I move to hit her in the arm, but she backs out of my reach. "What the hell is wrong with you? You don't just talk about that stuff kind of stuff in a room full of people."

"Technically, we're in a plane," she smirks. "Besides, they can't hear us. Most of them are too busy getting their crap together," she leans closer to me, "so are you going to?"

"I don't know. Maybe? Probably?" I can't believe I'm having this conversation right here. What if one of the other attendants hears me? "I'm not going to specifically plan for it. If it feels right, then we'll act on it. I'm not going to screw him just because. I need to know that he's not like most other men."

"That's good and all, but from what I can tell, he's a solid choice. I've been checking the gossip articles as much as you have, and anytime I've seen him mentioned he's been with that guy he usually travels with. Or he's with his team. There's definitely been a lack of scantily clad women. I think that means he's the real deal."

She has a point. I've been watching the articles like a hawk and nothing has shown up since we started dating.

'We'll see. I know he has to go to the team hotel for a meeting. That should give me enough time to go home and clean just in case."

"I don't see how your apartment could be dirty. You're almost never home."

"It's usually just dusting. But I need to make sure there's no dirty laundry on the bathroom floor."

"Seems legit," she nods in agreement. "Well, it's time to wish these passengers farewell. Well, most of them." The devilish quirk of her lips tells me she has no doubt in her mind that I'll be having sex tonight.

I roll my eyes and push past her. I can't even with this woman. I swear if I had an angel on one shoulder, she'd be the bad influence on the other, but I love her like a sister. Sometimes more than my actual sister. She's been there for me more times than I can count, and when I don't want her there.

I stand by the plane exit, waiting for the passengers to leave, offering goodbyes and hoping they have a great trip. Most of them are waiting for another plane to reach their destination, but some are here to take in the sights. Little as they may be.

As per usual, Bentley waits until he's the last one to get off the plane. "Are you ready for our date tonight?"

He slides his arm around my waist and pulls me close to him. He leans in for a kiss then stops, remembering I'm still on the clock. "Yes, I'm ready. I can meet you at the restaurant."

"Are you sure? I don't mind coming to get you first."

I shake my head before he can argue anymore. "I'm sure. It's dumb for you to pay to come to my place and then go right back downtown. There's no sense in it."

"Okay," he pulls back from me. "I'll see you in a few hours. Hopefully, this team meeting won't take too long."

Glancing around me, I make sure nobody is watching and I give him a quick peck. "I'll see you soon." He grabs the handle of his suitcase and makes his way down the narrow hall.

"Yeah," Lana whispers from right behind me. I jump. Where the hell did she come from? "You're totally getting laid tonight."

"Shut up." I don't say anything else. I grab my luggage and get off the plan. I don't care if she is right, she doesn't have to be all weird about it.

Our reservations are at a top end steakhouse. I told him I didn't need anything fancy, but he felt bad that we've only been eating fast food, or whatever the hotels offer. As far as going out is concerned, I'm a pretty simple girl. I don't need all the bells and whistles. As long as I'm enjoying my time with him, I'm perfectly happy.

I spot him as I push through the crowd of people. I can't believe so many people are braving the cold weather, but I get it. This is normal for us. Bentley is standing outside the restaurant door with a heavy jacket on. "Hey, you beat me here."

"I almost wish I hadn't. It's freezing out here," he says through shaky lips. I can almost hear his teeth chattering.

"It's not that bad out here." It will be later, though. We're supposed to get a wave of snow flurries overnight. Nothing brutal, but I'm not telling him that. I'm not sure he'll be able to handle it.

"Speak for yourself," he says as he pulls me close to him.

His lips cold against my cheek. "This Texas boy doesn't handle this weather well at all. Hell, it was still in the sixties when I got to the airport."

"We can go inside now. Then you won't be such a crybaby." My mouth spreads into a wide, teasing grin. "Besides, I'm hungry. I didn't have time to eat before I came."

"I'm not a crybaby. But yes, let's go. That meeting drained me." He pulls the door open wide and a blast of hot air hits us. He waits for me to go ahead of him, but stands in the doorway for longer than necessary.

"You know there's heat in here, right?"

"I don't know what you're talking about." Taking a step forward, he puts his arm around my shoulder and leads us to the host stand. A woman in a black shirt stands behind the podium and she's looking down at a seating chart. "Hi, we have a reservation for Bentley."

She doesn't even look up to greet us, instead she runs her fingers over the tablet in front of her, searching for our reservation. "Yes, I have you right here. If you'll follow me, I'll get you seated." She still hasn't bothered to make eye contact. It's a little annoying and reeks of poor customer service. My job is in this line of work and I always pay attention to the passengers who fly with us. Well, except Bentley. I tried my hardest not to notice him. It's good business and keeps people happy.

"She seems kind of rude," Bentley leans down and whispers in my ear. At least I'm not the only one that feels this way.

"I thought so, too. Maybe she's having a bad night?" I'm not sure why I'm making excuses for her, but a shitty day can definitely affect how you respond to people.

"Here we are," she finally looks up and smiles. Maybe

she heard us. "Your waiter should be with you shortly." She's already heading back to the stand before we seated.

"That felt odd," Bentley says as he pulls my chair out.

"I agree."

"Oh well, we're here now. Let's make the best of the rest of the night." He takes his jacket off, hanging it over the chair, and sits across from me. "What did you do when you got off work?"

"Not much," I shrug. "Cleaned the apartment and did some laundry. The usual when I get home from back-to-back flights."

"I don't see how you do it."

"Do what?" I'm looking over the menu while we wait on the server.

"Stay gone all the time." It's a question I've never been asked before. Few people care to know, or they think I'm living the dream. Jet Setting off to various locations and doing what I please. While most of it is true, it's also tiring. I've never mentioned to anyone else that I've been wanting to do something else for a while. Something that doesn't require me to be gone most of the time. It gets old coming home to an empty apartment, or only being home a day or two a week.

"It's not always easy. Especially with times like now." I set the menu down and continue, "Dating is the worst part of it unless you're also dating someone in the same line of work. But it's not much different for you, is it? You're away from home a lot when you play out of town."

"I'm still home a majority of the time. And there's off season when we rarely travel for the team." He pauses, as if he doesn't want to say what he's going to, but throws it out there, anyway. "Is that why you dated that pilot? Because he was in the same line of work?"

Honestly, I was wondering when this question would come up. He has to be wondering what happened. Especially after that awkward scene the day I met him. "Sort of. I mean, I was attracted to him, along with all the other flight attendants. Being with him for that brief time almost ruined my friendship with Lana. Luckily, she was there for me when it all ended. I thought I would be the one that changed him and made him settle down. Turns out...I wasn't." I take a deep breath, knowing what I'm about to admit will be a punch to the gut for him. "It's why I was so resistant to dating you."

The waiter chooses that moment to approach our table. "Can I interest you in one of our wines?"

He nods to me, and I look over the list, not really paying attention to the selections. I point to one, and I have no clue what it is, but the description says it's sweet. The waiter nods and disappears again. For such a fancy restaurant, the service is slow.

"What do I have to do with him?"

"You're a lot alike. After you approached me for a date, I looked you up. I needed to know what I would be getting myself into." This may hurt him just as much as the previous statement, but he should know why I had my reservations. "All that came up was pictures of you leaving clubs, and bars, with various women. There was never a repeat. That isn't something I wanted for myself."

"What changed your mind?" He leans across the table, trying to get closer despite the flowers taking up space in the middle. He wants in on the secret of why.

"Seeing you with that little girl." The memory makes me smile. It was probably the sweetest thing I've ever seen. This big sports dude admitting his own fears to a child to make her feel better. "And the way you always help people with their luggage after a flight. Someone that selfish wouldn't go out of their way to help people." I reach across the table and place my hand on top of his. "That is why I gave you a chance."

"I can't promise that I won't piss you off at times but I'll do my best." Bentley turns his hand over and grips mine in his. As much as this conversation wasn't what I expected, his hands are strong and warm. I expected them to be sweaty after all the questions he had. He's as cool as a cucumber.

I laugh as the waiter comes back with the wine. "I think you pissed me off more when you were chasing me so hard. I kept waiting for you to back off and determine I wasn't worth the effort." Or tired of wanting something that wasn't attainable. Though, he knocked that out of the water with his dates. I'm happy I gave him a chance.

"I've already told you; you are worth so much more than you realize." Excuse me while I melt into a puddle of goo. He's told me once before, but I've never had anyone try to accommodate my life so well. Not Carter. Hell, not even my parents. He wins on that aspect alone.

"Good, that means Lana won't have to kick your ass if this all falls apart." I wink at him before taking a sip of the wine. His eyes lock on my lips touching the glass, and I want to know what's going through his head. If the heat and intensity of his gaze are any indication, then it's what else he'd like my lips wrapped around.

I almost spit out my wine the second the thought hits my brain and end up choking. "Ma'am, are you okay?" The waiter bends down until we're at eye level with each other.

I wipe my hand across my chin and nod my head. "Yeah, it just went down the wrong pipe."

"We can leave if we need to," Bentley offers.

"No," I wave him off. "Let's order our food. I'm fine, I promise."

"If you say so." He turns his attention to the waiter and places his order. I don't even know what I want but I just say whatever he's getting. "You're putting a lot of trust in my food choices."

"You haven't steered me wrong yet. Besides, this place is a little stuffy for my tastes."

"Mine, too," he agrees. "I wanted to do something special for you, though."

"I appreciate it." I tap my finger against my chin. I know what I'm going to say, but I don't know what his response will be. "Do you maybe want to go back to my place after dinner?"

"See," he grins. "You should have led with that. We wouldn't be in this overpriced restaurant if you had."

"And that is why I didn't." I hope I'm not making a colossal mistake. I don't remember the last guy I brought home. Carter never even saw where I lived since most of our hookups happened while we were traveling. This is the next step in seeing where things go with me and Bentley. I also know we'll end up in my bed. I've seen him in practice clothes and casual wear. But the slacks and button-up shirt he's wearing right now would look so much better on my floor.

NINETEEN

Bentley

The blast of frosty air as we walk out of the restaurant is enough to make me wish I was back in Texas. It gets cold there, but not like this. Tiny white flurries fall from the sky and I can't deny how beautiful it is. Snow rarely happens in Austin, and when it does everyone loses their minds. Nobody can drive in it and most schools shut down for that reason. Living in this kind of cold is not my idea of a good time.

I wrap my arms around Jolene and pull her closer to me, her back against my chest. It does nothing to warm me up, but hopefully it gives her some warmth. "Do we need to grab a cab or Uber?" The small alcove in front of the door protects us from some of the wind.

"Actually, I drove." She looks up and hits her forehead on my chin. "I'm parked right around the corner."

"Lead the way." We walk for a few feet with her still wrapped in my arms in front of me. It's difficult. We look like waddling ducks.

Finally, she swoops out from under my arm. "It'll probably be faster if we walk side by side."

"Oh, uh, yeah. You're right." The loss of contact sucks, and the bitter cold hits me in the chest. It'd be wrong of me to suggest that she come back and protect me from it, right?

"You can hold me again while we wait for the car to warm up," she winks. It's a small consolation, but worth the wait. "Let's go." She grabs my hand and pulls me behind her.

We aren't strolling along at a leisurely pace. It's a quick walk and I'm worried I'll slip and bust my ass. Because that is what women find attractive. I concentrate with everything I have and will my feet to stay steady. There are always chances of slipping in sweat when on the court, but you can see those glistening spots on the floor. The lighting is dim from the snow flurries and shadows of others passing by us on the sidewalk. I can't see any signs of slickness. Let's hope that means nothing has accumulated and we make it to her car safely.

Rounding the corner, she picks up her pace. "My car is right over there."

"You know this isn't a race, right?" The flurries are getting bigger and hit me in the face. It wouldn't be so bad if they'd stop landing in my fucking eyes.

She laughs as we near what I assume is her car. "I'm just trying to protect your Southern ass. I know you don't like cold weather."

We stop at the driver side door of an older model sedan. I can't tell what kind it is, but I know from the body style it's almost a decade old. She unlocks it and I move to open the door for her. Slipping on a small patch of ice I didn't see; I end up pressing her against the car. Her breath comes out in soft pants, small white clouds leaving her mouth on every exhalation. Eyes wide, her gaze meets mine and despite the cold and the fact I can't feel my fingers, I lean down and press my lips to hers.

She doesn't pull away. Her hands trapped between us grasp onto my jacket, yanking me closer. My tongue swirls with hers and I use the top of her car to support my weight. I lose all track of time as she tries to pull me flush against her body. The thickness of my jacket keeps us from that.

I move one of my hands and tangle it in her hair, grateful that she wears it down when she's not at work. A moan escapes into my mouth as I deepen the kiss. She breaks away, placing small kisses along my neck. Teasing me the way I teased her when she was in Austin. Dammit, this isn't fair. Not when I can't strip her out of her clothes in privacy.

"Get a room," someone from a couple of rows down yells, breaking the bubble we've been in for the past few minutes.

Jolene pulls away from me and looks down at her hands gripping my shirt. "I'm so sorry. I'm not sure what got into me."

Running a finger down the side of her face, I lift her chin until her eyes meet mine. "Never apologize for that. But maybe we can go back to your place now. We'll have privacy there."

She nods and turns to get in the car. I wait until she's settled in her seat and close the door. I'd offer to drive, but I'm one of the people that doesn't do well with wintry weather. I round the car and slide into the passenger seat. Leaning over, I kiss her one more time before putting my seatbelt on. "Let's get out of here. I have plans for you."

A sly smile crosses her face as she puts the car in reverse

and merges into traffic. I'm going to make her forget every man before me.

The drive doesn't take long. With as many people as we saw on the sidewalks, I figured traffic would be horrible. Apparently, those who were going to get out and about already are, and everyone else has stayed in.

Jolene pulls into a parking garage and parks close to the elevators. "We're here," she squeaks out nervously, but doesn't reach for the door.

"Are we going to get out, or stay in the car? Don't get me wrong, I'm happy to be anywhere you are, but inside might be more comfortable... and warmer." I'm only giving her a hard time. Even if I have plans, of every way I want to claim her, she's still skittish. The only reason I know she wants more is because she initiated the kiss in the parking lot. She pulled me closer and made me lose all sense of reality.

"Yeah," she reaches for the door handle before I can get out to open it for her. She waits until I'm beside her before walking toward the door next to the elevators.

Despite the frigid air and the promise of warmth her apartment brings, I pull her to a stop. She gasps as I run a finger along her jawline, and brush kisses along the same path. A small reminder of what's coming.

Her breathing picks up and she shudders at my touch. "Let's get inside." This time we're rushing for completely different reasons. A part of me wants to scoop her into my arms and carry her to our destination, if only to speed things up. But I have no idea where to go, and I don't want to freak her out.

She leads me down a hallway by the edge of my jacket,

then turns down another one. I'm nothing more than a puppy, eagerly following her, and waiting for my treat. Stopping in front of her door, she fumbles with her keys. I slide my arm around her waist and under her jacket, caressing her waistline through the thin red fabric of her dress. Her keys fall from her hand and she mutters a curse. "We will never make it inside if you keep distracting me."

I pause in my teasing to pick up the keys and place them in her outstretched hand. "You've been distracting me all damn night," I whisper in her ear.

She shudders against me and shakes her head. "We'll cause a scene if we don't make it inside, then I'll have to move from embarrassment." Finding the correct keys, she slides it into the lock.

"Fine," I pout and slide my hand over hers. "But the minute that door closes behind us...you are mine." The last part is a growl and I hope she knows just how serious I am.

Instead of answering me, she turns the key and pushes the door open. I take that as all the invitation I need. But Jolene surprises me. She yanks the key out of the door and turns to face me. Her hands reach for the lapels of my jacket and she pulls be toward her, closing the distance between us. Walking backward, she tugs me along, her lips inching toward mine.

As soon as I clear the door, I kick it closed with my foot. I pause to lock the door behind me, but she yanks me forward. "Don't worry about that. The only person who barges in unannounced is Lana, and she's been warned not to show up."

"So, you planned to seduce me all along," I chuckle. "And here I thought it was the other way around."

"Shut up and kiss me already." Who am I to disappoint? I slam my mouth into hers. Our hands are busy, trying to get our jackets off of each other without breaking contact. It's not an easy feat, but we manage to shrug our jackets off with our lips still fused together.

Now that the bulk between us is gone, I can do what I wish. I pick her up, her legs wrapping around my waist. She gasps as my hardness hits her center. "We should go to the bedroom," she pants.

"Tell me where it is." She tries to slide down, but I grasp her ass, keeping her in place. "Just tell me." I don't want to lose contact. Lose the feel of her body pressed against mine.

"Straight down the hall. It's the door at the end." She clings to me, pressing feverish kisses against my throat. Arms secured around me so she doesn't fall. Not like I would let that happen. In less than a minute we're in her room, and I place her right beside her bed.

Her hand reaches for the strap of her dress, but I grab it before she even has a hold of it. "Don't. I want to do that." As much as I've always enjoyed the rush of getting a woman into my bed, I want to take my time with her. She's not like the other women, and I don't want to treat her like she is.

Her cheeks pinken and she steps toward me, hands outstretched. Her fingers fumble with the buttons on my shirt. One by one the buttons come apart, my undershirt exposed with each one. Her warm breath hits my chest as she comes closer, sliding my shirt off my shoulders.

The moment feels surreal, and like so much more than just sex. I honestly can't remember the last time a woman has undressed me. Or if it's ever happened before. I relish the time she's taking to pay attention to my body. Taking her time. Torturing me in the best way possible.

She reaches her hand under my shirt, tracing the muscles as she lifts it up and up. I hurry the process and reach behind my head, pulling it off in one swift movement.

"Somebody is impatient," she smirks as she trails her hands down my chest, then my stomach, before stopping at the top of my pants. With one finger she unbuttons them, and excruciatingly slowly pulls the zipper down. Grabbing the waistband of both my pants and boxers, she slides them down my legs, gasping as my cock springs free.

She sits on the edge of the bed, staring at me. I feel insecure, completely undressed and vulnerable to her gaze. Wondering how much of me she's truly seeing. Not just the superficial stuff. My muscled body, or scars from falling off my bike and trying crazy ass stunts on the court. But the fear I have that this is something real. Something I've never had before. That she's made me want her for more than a couple of nights of fun.

I grab her hands until she's standing again. My hand reaches for the bottom of her dress, and I slowly lift it up. Running my fingers over her soft skin, never breaking contact, until I pull it over her head and throw it on the floor behind us.

All she's left in are her lacy bra and panties, and her heels. "You are a sight for sore eyes."

She bursts out laughing. Not exactly the reaction I was expecting considering I'm buck naked and trying to be sweet. "Sorry. I just never understood that phrase, and it's kind of cheesy."

"Okay," I breathe out. "You are stunning. Every. Single. Inch." I drive the point home by tracing the outline of her bra until I reach the back and undo the clasp.

"You're pretty good at that." Her voice is shaky. I'm not sure if it's from nerves or the fact that I can take a bra off one-handed in less than thirty seconds. A result of lots of practice, but she doesn't need to have that confirmed. Not now, and not ever.

"Mhm," I mumble. She starts to take her panties off, but I stop her. "That's my job."

I ease her onto her bed until she's lying down. Her long brown hair fans out above her, and she looks ethereal. I study every inch of exposed skin. Tonight, will be one she never forgets.

TWENTY

Jolene

BENTLEY TOWERS OVER ME, domineering and unafraid to take what he wants. He's most definitely the wolf and I'm the prey. I watch him taking in my body on full display. Yearning for something I've been holding out on giving him. The reward at the end of the chase. I wasn't putting this off because I wanted to tease him. That would be cruel, and I'm not that sort of woman. I wanted to make sure it was right...for both of us. That I could trust him. I haven't seen his face grace the font of a tabloid in weeks. At least, not with another woman. It's mostly him hanging out with teammates or shooting hoops with Derrick. That's how I know he's trustworthy, and tonight will be perfect.

He leans over me until his face is mere inches away from mine. "Are you still good? I don't want to stop what we've started, but I will if you have any doubts."

His fingers brush a stray hair off my forehead and the gentleness turns me on more than when he picked me up and carried me to my room. The soft side that he doesn't show anyone else is precisely why I'm falling for him. "I'm good."

Nodding his understanding, he kisses along my jawline, pausing to nip at my ear. He gently sucks on my lobe and heat rushes south. Who would have known I'm a sucker for my ears being played with? I turn my head until my lips brush against his. "Kiss me."

He doesn't hesitate. His mouth melds to mine, and it's pure perfection. It's as if my lips were made for his. They make me forget all the rejection in my past. The hurt so many, especially those who were supposed to love me unconditionally, have caused me to disappear. All that matters is right now, with him.

His mouth breaks away from mine and works down my neck, settling on my right nipple. He bites down. Not too hard, but hard enough to no longer know the difference between pain and pleasure.

I squirm under the attention his mouth and tongue give me. His dick twitches with the friction. "Stop torturing me already," I all but pant.

He doesn't respond, but I can feel him smile against my skin. He gives attention to the other nipple, but nowhere near as much as he did the first. My body is on fire and he hasn't even entered me yet. I swear if he doesn't do something soon, I'm going to scream out of frustration.

I move my hand to his head and tangle my fingers in his hair. Maybe if I guide him further down, he'll take the hint. It's been months since I've been with anyone, and I know I will go off like a firework at the slightest touch.

Finally, he works his way down. His tongue gliding a patch down my stomach. He reaches one hand up to pinch my nipple, and the other to my warm center. Feeling how much I want him through the lace fabric. "I think you're almost ready for me." His voice is gruff. As if it's taking everything in him not to devour me. His breath against my thighs sends shivers through my body. I'm going to lose it before he's done anything. This is one of those times I wish foreplay didn't exist. The wait until the main attraction is almost painful.

Using his teeth, he pulls down the edge of my panties and shimmies them down my legs. I start to kick my heels off, but he places a hand on my foot. A silent command to leave them on. That's kind of weird, but whatever floats his boat.

Before I can ask what's taking so long, I feel his breath against my clit. He doesn't start off slow, either. He's done taking his time, and within minutes...I'm seeing stars. Son of a bitch, I should have listened to Lana all those months ago and had fun until I found someone to be serious with. Because I feel like I did in my younger days every slight touch would make me explode. He doesn't relent, though. Only grips my thighs, pulling me closer to him. And I'm left riding wave after wave of ecstasy.

I can't take anymore and I push his head back, needing a break from the onslaught of feeling. He arches an eyebrow and stares at me from the edge of the bed. "Had enough already?"

"It's, um, been a while." Embarrassment rushes through me, and I'm sure my face is bright red. Even though I'm far from being a virgin, I feel like I'm at a different level than he is when it comes to sex.

"It's all good. We can take this as slow or fast as you want." He climbs onto the bed next to me and pulls me closer to him.

"I'm okay now. That was just intense." He's obviously mastered the art of going down on women. While a part of me is jealous, I know that none of the women before me matter. At least, not right now.

"Do you want to keep going?" He sounds sincere, but I know that stopping now would be torture for him. And me, if I'm being honest. I need to feel him inside me. To connect with him physically the way we connect on our virtual dates and when we see each other.

"Yes," I nod. "There are condoms in the top drawer of the nightstand." I point above me to the furniture in question. Even though it's the only one by my bed.

"So, you were prepared for tonight." It's not a question. I may act like I don't want this to only be physical, but I can't deny the way he makes me feel. How he makes me want more. He reaches over us and grabs the square foil packet out of the drawer. "What if it's not big enough?"

"Someone is a little sure of themselves," I wave him off. "We'll manage because as much as I want you right now, you aren't coming near me without protection."

"I don't know if I should be offended, or not," he scrunches his eyebrows together. "As if I'd ever do anything that made you uncomfortable."

"Dude, you pursued me after I told you I didn't want to date. Then, you conspire with my best friend to get the outcome you want." I roll my eyes at him, "I don't think there's much you wouldn't do to get what you wanted."

"I may be confident in myself, but I'm not an asshole." He says all this while rolling the condom over his erection. It looks snug, but as long as it doesn't break...we're good. "Now," he leans over and places kiss after kiss along my shoulder. "Where were we?"

I shiver under the feel of his lips on my skin. The way he runs his hands down my body until he finds what he's looking for. "Yeah," I squeak out. "I think that's exactly where we were."

"You know, I think you're right." He moves until he's looming over me, between my legs, just one push from being inside me. He slides forward until the tip of his cock is lined up with me, but he doesn't go any further. "You sure?"

"If you don't do something soon, I'm going to take care of it myself." That's all the permission he needs. He slams into me and my entire body ignites. He fills me completely, stretching me with each push. He wraps one arm around me, bringing me closer to him, until I can feel him deep inside me. Claiming me inch by inch.

"Bentley," his name is a whisper on my lips. That spurs him on. Faster and faster until all I see are stars as I come undone around him. Shuddering as the final throes of ecstasy leave my body.

Within minutes he's gripping my body harder than before. His fingers wrapping in my hair, pulling my head back until he stiffens. His cock pulsing inside me as he finds his release.

Gently, he frees his hand from my hair and lowers me to the bed. I'm not sure what he sees on my face, but he asks, "Are you okay?"

"Yeah," I nod. At least, I think I am. It's been months since I've been with anyone, and he was my re-introduction into having a sex life again. He's made it impossible for others to live up to him. And I'm not complaining one little bit.

He rolls off of me before getting off the bed and going to the restroom. I can do nothing but lay in pure bliss. Absolutely nothing can bring me down from the high I feel right now. He comes back to the bed, a knowing smirk on his face. "Are you ready for bed?"

All I can do is nod and pull the blanket out from underneath me. He slides in behind me, wraps his arm around my waist and pulls me flush with him. The contact alone is enough to make me want more. The way his hand slides from my waist and down my hip, back and forth, lets me know he does, too. I can already tell it's going to be a long night. I don't know when we'll actually let our eyes close for the night, but I know I will drink in every moment I have with him before he leaves.

Light streaming from the window wakes me up. Wait, why is there light coming through? Blackout curtains aren't supposed to allow that to happen. I know for a fact they were closed before we fell asleep last night.

I swing my arm behind me, feeling for the body that should be there. That's supposed to be there, but it's missing. The spot he was lying in is still warm. That's a good sign. At least I know he didn't sneak out in the wee hours of the morning once I fell asleep. But that doesn't mean he didn't just do it. But why open the curtains? To be an asshole?

Sounds come from the kitchen. Dishes clattering together and water running from the sink. Relieved he didn't bail on me; I sink further into my bed and pull the blanket over my head to block the sunlight. Last night was perfect. From the dinner to the sex. All of it. I've had amazing dates before, but this one...it puts all others to shame. This is the first time, despite knowing how badly he wanted me, I had someone truly show their appreciation of me in their life. He treated me like a goddess and if the noise in the apartment is any indication, he plans to continue that.

I have no clue what he's putting together, though. I haven't had a chance to get groceries. I wasn't playing when I told Lana I was coming home to clean like crazy. My refrigerator is almost never stocked. The food would go bad before I have a chance to eat it, and it's just easier to grab take out when I'm home.

"Are you awake?" From the sound of his voice, he's standing at the doorway.

"If I said no, would it make a difference?" I slide the blanket down from my face and glance over at him. Holy shit. Bentley with his shirt off, in nothing but his boxers and his hair messy from sleep, is a glorious thing to wake up to. Let's not forget the two plates he's holding. I wouldn't mind waking up to this more often.

"Not really," he shrugs and steps toward the bed. He sets the plate down at the foot of the bed before gently climbing in beside me. "I was going to make you breakfast, but your fridge is stocked about as well as mine. It's a good thing you had frozen breakfast burritos."

"Frozen food is about the only thing I keep on hand." I attempt to shrug but get tangled in the blanket. "I can't even cook very well."

"I guess we'll starve then," he grins. "I can't cook either. But I have a secret weapon."

It's good to know I'm not the only one who struggles with cooking, but I need to know what this secret weapon is. "And, what's that?"

"My mom lives less than twenty minutes from me. All I have to do is show up at her house for dinner."

"That's wrong on so many levels. How are you going to make your mom cook for you?"

"I don't make her do anything. She's stubborn as hell, but I'm not going to turn down the offer to go over there for good food." He grabs the plates before pulling me close to him. "Now, eat. I have a surprise for you."

"Unless it's a repeat of last night...I don't want it." I snuggle into his side and bask in the feel of being next to him. Of being with a man that doesn't try to tell me what to do, or how to act. Of a man that has done all he can to prove that I'm the only one he has eyes for.

"That can be arranged." He mutters into my hair and pokes me playfully in the side. "But no, that's not it."

"It's not nice to poke people," I grumble. "Why can't you just tell me now?"

"Because I'm hungry, and if you want a repeat, you're going to need your strength."

"Fine." I may be pouting but so what. I don't understand what's so secretive that he can't spill the beans while we eat. I grab the plate off his lap and take a bite of the burrito. It's already lost some of its heat and the eggs are rubbery, but if he wants me to eat, then I will. After swallowing, I put the burrito down. "There, I ate. Now, tell me."

"Fine. Since you're so impatient." That last part is barely audible, but I still make it out. "I got you, and Lana, front row tickets to the game tonight. You said you've never been to a game, and I want you there."

Holy crap. That had to have been insanely expensive. I'm sure he has perks when they are playing in their home stadium, but I'm not sure how that works when they travel. "Bentley, that's too much."

"You don't need to worry about that," he taps me on the nose. "All that matters to me is that you get to experience the game up close and personal. Just be on the lookout because there are times the ball, or players, will end up in that area."

"Soooo, you're putting me in harm's way." I side-eye him. Unsure if that's the best decision. Maybe we would be better higher up.

"It doesn't happen often. I only wanted to give you a heads up to not freak out. Most of the players try their best to avoid it at all costs."

"That's good to know," I mutter. "What does one wear to a basketball game?"

"Clothes, usually." He narrowly dodges my elbow to his ribs. "Just jeans and a t-shirt. Nothing fancy. Well, except I also have a jersey for you."

My heart flutters in my chest. It might not mean anything, but in my mind it's him showing the world that he's with me. I know that's ridiculous because other people will undoubtedly be wearing one with his name on it, but it doesn't stop me from hoping that's the case. It's safe to say that I've one hundred percent fallen off the deep end with him. "Where is it?"

"It's at the hotel," he chuckles. "Lana will pick you up and then meet Jordan's wife there before heading to the game."

"Do I get a say in any of this?"

"Not really." He picks up the plates of nearly untouched frozen burritos and puts them on the nightstand. "I already cleared it with Lana. I didn't want you to go alone and feel out of your element."

He may be a badass on the court and in bed, but he really does have a sweet side. Not many men would think about that stuff. Yep, I'm totally a goner. "Since the plan was already made without my input, I know a way you can make it up to me..."

I let the sentence trail off, hoping he gets the hint. An eyebrow raise is the only response. Fine, it looks like I'll have to take matters into my own hands. I push the blanket off and straddle him...I can seduce him just as much as he does me.

TWENTY-ONE

Bentley

As HAPPY AS I thought I was flitting from woman to woman, nothing compares to being with Jolene. Well... almost. Seeing her in the front row, wearing my jersey, is pretty damn amazing.

She looks like she's having a good time. At least, from what I can tell when I glance over. I wish I could be on the sideline with her, explaining the game as the plays happen. But I'm right here, on the court, where I belong. Hell, I'm not even sure what I would do if I wasn't playing ball. I only know it would revolve around sports somehow.

"Yo, Bentley," Jordan smacks my arm. The sounds of the game come flooding back in. The people in the stands yelling and cheering for their teams. "Get your head in the game. We aren't ahead enough for you to be giving puppy dog eyes to your girl."

"I don't know what you're talking about," I huff. "I don't give that look to anyone." Except I am. And now I feel like a hypocrite after giving Derrick hell while I was still at Hill-town U.

"Dude, I know that look," he glances over at the woman who has made me want to give relationships an actual shot. "It's the look I still give my wife."

He's not lying. I've caught them staring at each other like they've just started dating. It's gross and hopeful at the same time. What has happened to me? I'm not that guy. The one who settles down with a nice girl and wants to wake up to the same person every morning. Except, I am. Jolene makes me want more than casual relationships and hookups. It's like this whole new version of me is opening up. I'm not sure what to do about it.

Nope, right now isn't the time to think about that. I need to get my head on straight and focus. We have a game to win. I can't do that if I let the beautiful brunette steal my attention every single time we call a timeout, or I'm on the bench. My team needs me to help them snag this game. Each win brings us closer and closer to the champion round. It doesn't matter what it takes, I'll make sure we get there.

The final buzzer goes off signaling our victory. The other team fought us all the way to the end, but we came out on top. Instead of going to the guys like I normally would, I head straight toward the stands. Jolene is on her feet next to Jordan's wife and Lana. The smile she is wearing is huge, and I'm happy to know that she was here cheering for me. I want this to be more than a onetime thing. I want her at all of my games, but that's not going to happen anytime soon. Not unless she changes her career. I may be a selfish asshole sometimes. But...I'm not the sort of person to force another to quit their job or change the entire life direction based on what I want. In my opinion, that would make me no better than my father, and that is the last person I want to emulate.

The moment she sees me, she stops cheering and walks toward me. I meet her halfway, sweeping her off the floor and twirling her around. "So how was your first game experience?"

She's laughing, and the sound fills me with joy. Knowing I'm the one that caused it. "It was great. And even better, you won." I feel her gaze shift as she looks over my shoulder. "Um, Bentley. There are cameras pointed directly at us."

I set her down, and she buries her face into my sweaty jersey. That has got to be disgusting, but she's obviously not ready for any sort of attention from the media. "Go back over there with Lana, and I'll deal with this."

"Just don't put my name out there. I'm not with you to become famous or anything, and I'd rather not have that focus." I didn't even think about that when I came over here. All that was on my mind was getting to her.

"Okay. I won't say who you are." As soon as her back is to me, I turn around to face the reporters.

"Bentley, Bentley." My name is shouted from four different directions, and I'm not sure who to address first. Most of the fans have cleared the stands and all that's left are the reporters and players. Some of my own teammates are pulled into interviews all around the court. One reporter from a smaller sports network stands out because she's not fighting for my attention. I don't know much about her, but I've seen her around here and there. I walk toward her, and she grins, knowing she played her cards right. By being patient and not loud or obnoxious has led me to her camera.

"Hi, Bentley. I'm Savannah with Sports Network. As the only rookie this year for the Austin Rattlers, you're garnering a lot of attention. What does it feel like gaining popularity so quickly?"

"I'm not sure how I feel, honestly. I didn't get drafted to the team because I wanted to be famous. I worked my ass off to make sure this team picked me up because I love the sport. I love playing for my home city. I do the same thing I've done since I was a kid." None of this is a lie. I've given so many variations of this response, it comes out of my mouth without much thought.

She leans closer to me with her microphone. As if she's conspiring with me. "And what's that?"

"I go out there and play. I give it my everything and do the best I can to support my teammates."

"Pretty soon you'll be surpassing your teammates." She winks at me like it's a secret. I will outperform some of the other players. But it's not my intention to brag about it. They are still my teammates, and we're a unit. Being a dick, on camera, isn't going to win me any favors with Coach, or the guys.

Shaking my head, I answer, "That's not what I'm after. You can't get on that court and win a game without the other players."

Her smile widens, and I'm a little nervous about the sudden gleam in her eye. Maybe it was a bad decision to pick her to talk to out of all the reporters, but it's too late to worry about that now. "Well, I can't wait to see what you do with your career."

"Thanks, I'm excited to see what the Rattlers can do this season."

"If it's anything like what you all have done, I know you'll be headed to the Championships." She raises an eyebrow, and I'm the only one that can see it because she is off-camera. I have a feeling I'm not going to like what comes out of her mouth next. "Maybe that pretty young lady over there will join you on your journey."

Yup, she's just like the gossip magazines. Rather than focusing on the game, she's doing all she can to pry into my life. I'm not going to give her the satisfaction of getting a peek into my personal life. That's nobody's business but my own. "Well, the Championship is what we're working toward."

Rather than give her a chance to dig a little more, I turn my back toward her and head to the locker rooms. This is what Jordan has been trying to prepare me for. Why he's tried to be such a parent-like figure and lead me toward better choices.

Speak of the devil, he's waiting for me at the end of the hallway leading toward the locker room. "You did good out there."

"Is that what it was like when you first started playing? They did everything they can to delve into your personal life?" I've done plenty of after game interviews, and that's the most personal it's ever gotten.

"Some of them, yes. But most of the reporters want to know about the game." He nods to the one who was just talking to me, and who is still staring at me. "You have to watch out for that one, though. She likes to act like she's following your career, but all she does is stir up drama."

"How do you know that?" Not that I'm arguing. I saw the look in her eye right before she decided to ask me about Jolene.

"She hasn't done anything to me personally, but some of the guys on the other teams say she's a problem."

"That's good to know. Now let's go get cleaned up and

take our ladies out for a night on the town." It's a well-deserved reward after the way we played tonight.

He slaps me on the back and chuckles. "Look at you. All serious in your relationship."

"Shut up, man." We both turn and walk down the hall-way. I'm definitely going to keep my eye on this new reporter chick because I smell trouble. I'm not afraid to deal with whatever comes my way, but I don't want Jolene pulled into it.

I barely have my shirt over my head when my phone rings against the metal locker. I know it's not Jolene because she's waiting with Lana and Jordan's wife, but I have no idea who else it could be. Unless Derrick needs another pick me up, of course. I don't bother glancing at the screen when I finally answer, "Hello?" It's probably him, calling to talk shop about the game that just ended.

"Who is this girl you were with all over TV?" Shit, I completely forgot Mom watches all the games. I didn't think about the cameras or where they would shift their attention when I wasn't doing what I normally do. I probably should have brought up Jolene a long time ago. I wanted to make sure things were going to work out before I brought her into my family.

"Hi, Mom," I try to sound more cheerful than I do, but I'm pretty sure it's not working. "That was my, um, girlfriend."

I hear her gasp on the other end of the phone. Holy shit, I think I just gave my mom a heart attack. "You mean to tell me you have a girlfriend and you haven't told us about her?"

"I never told you about my other girlfriends." I use the term girlfriend loosely. I haven't had one since high school.

"Don't be smart with me," she admonishes. "I know good and well those other girls are not your girlfriend. I'm not stupid. So, who is this new girl?"

I don't like the way she says "new girl". I know that's my own fault because I go through them so quickly, but it sounds dirty now that I'm in a relationship. "Her name is Jolene. I was going to tell you about her when I came over for dinner, but surprise."

I hear snickers from behind me, and I turn to see who exactly is enjoying the show. Freaking Jordan and Ross. Of course, they are here to witness this. Because that's the luck I have. They will no doubt give me shit about this for weeks to come. Jordan knows just how well my mom is at putting me in my place and wanting to know all the details.

Gabby is in the background, and I know my mom just put it on speakerphone. "So, you finally found someone who will last more than one night?"

"Gabby," Mom chastises, "that wasn't very nice."

"Well, it's not like it's not true."

This, ladies and gentlemen, is why I don't call them all the time. And why I don't tell them anything that's going on until I know it's a sure thing. I love my sister. She has been my rock, but she also knows how to press my buttons. "Actually, for your information. We have been dating for over a month?"

"Woah, look at you go."

Should I tell them now that I am planning to bring her down? Or should I leave it a surprise? Fuck it, I will tell them now. "As soon as her schedule allows, I plan on bringing her to meet you all."

"What is it that she does?" My mom sounds cautious. As

if Jolene may be in some wayward business. And she's digging. It's nothing that I didn't expect because she's nosy as hell and tries to be in my business all the time.

"She's a flight attendant. Her schedule doesn't always match up with when I have a game or when I have to travel. But we will figure something out."

My sister snorts, and I don't want to know what she's thinking. Unfortunately for me, she tells me anyway. "Sounds like the perfect woman for you, Bentley. You get to see her when you want and still be able to have all the fun you want on the side. Isn't that what life is all about now that you've become a famous basketball player?"

I don't know what crawled up her ass, but this definitely isn't a conversation to be having in front of our mother. "For your information I haven't seen anyone besides her in a long time. She has her own issues to work through, and I'm not adding to them. If you can't stop being a bitch, then I'm not going to bring her around at all."

"Aye dios mio," Mom sighs. "What am I gonna do with the two of you? You are both adults, and it's time to act like it. I can't believe I still have to break up your fights at this age."

She's right, and I know that. But Gabby needs to get off my case. It's not like I flaunted my past discretions in front of her. Hell, that was the whole reason I never took them around family. I didn't want to introduce them to somebody that wasn't going to be around long. "I'm sorry, Mom." I rub my hand across my forehead, frustrated with the way this conversation has ended up. Even though I'm not the one who started. "I need to go. We have to be out of the locker room soon."

"Okay. I love you, Mijo. And I can't wait to meet Jolene." I hear the smile in her voice and know that she means it.

"Thanks Ma, I love you, too." As much as it sucks that me and my sister fight over this one thing, she'll come around. She will love Jolene just as much as I'm beginning to. Now, I just have to bring up to Jolene that she needs to meet my mom soon. That should be loads of fun.

TWENTY-TWO

Jolene

Tonight, has been more fun than I've had in a while. Lana and I showed Bentley, Jordan, his wife, and Ross some of our favorite places. From the pizza joint down the street from the stadium to the bar we frequent. It was amazing to show him my city. The place I've called home since I left my parents' house.

Now, though...my feet are killing me. After being on flights all week, and the late night with Bentley last night, I can hear my bed calling me. It's too bad that's not the bed I'm going to tonight. Or maybe not?

Bentley reaches for my hand as the elevator doors open. Everyone else has gone to their respective rooms, and Lana headed home after the bar. Which was kind of odd since she's usually a night owl? I didn't miss the looks her and Ross were giving each other. There has to be something there. Who knows? I could be reading into something that doesn't exist. Especially since I'm caught up in my own euphoria with Bentley.

As soon as we're inside the box and the doors close, he pulls me to me. His arms wrap around my waist. "Are you sure you don't want to go home tonight?"

"Yeah," I nod. "It's late. Besides, you're here and I'd much rather be with you." Gah, that sounds so mushy. Like something a teenager would say on a date with her first actual boyfriend. He makes me feel that way, though. Everything around us doesn't exist. It's just me and him, and all the fucked up things that screw with our hearts. It's not impossible to overcome, but we've torn down each other's walls. He knows about my shitty family, the horrible idea that was Carter, and that I'm not a flashy girl. And yet...he still hasn't walked away. He hasn't given any sign that I'm too much trouble even with me being states away from him. That speaks more to his genuine character than anything I've read. Or the cocky, self-assured persona he has on the court. We're more alike than I think either of us has realized.

"That's good to know." He bends down, blocking the already dim lighting in the elevator, and brushes his lips across mine. The kiss isn't rushed, or hurried. Nothing like the frantic pace we had last night. No, it's the exact opposite. Soft. Gentle. Promising me he's all in. That he's willing to do whatever it takes to make sure things between us work. It's reassuring, knowing he seems to feel the same way I feel about him.

I lean into the kiss, letting him know I trust him. As soon as the elevator doors open, he's backing me out, our lips never parting. As awkward as it is to walk backward, not knowing how far we are going, I don't pull away. I don't break the kiss. I meld with him completely until we come to a stop and he moves one hand to fumble in his back pocket.

"Damn it," he mumbles against my lips before pulling

back. "Why is it so hard to get your wallet out of your back pocket?"

"I don't know," I lean against the door we stopped in front of. "Maybe it's because your jeans are so damn tight that it would take a force of nature to pull it out."

He looks down at the jeans in question. "You don't like them?"

That doesn't deserve an answer, but I give it to him, anyway. "I do. But it is making it take longer to get into the room," I pause for a second, "and so does sitting outside your room talking about your clothing. It'd be a lot better if we were inside and they were on the floor."

His mouth drops open. I guess he wasn't expecting me to say that. It's not like I'm a prude or anything, but I can see why he might be surprised by my comment. "I guess we better remedy that." He finally gets the wallet out of his pocket, and searches for the key card. He waves it in front of the door, but the light stays a steady red. "You've got to be kidding me," he groans.

"Did you have it in the little paper sleeve while it was in your wallet?" I'm ninety percent sure I know what happened, and he's not going to like the answer.

"I'm not sure?" It comes out as a question, and I have my answer.

"Are you sure we're at the right room?" Might as well, figure that out while we're at it.

"Yes," he nods emphatically. "We definitely have the right door. What does that have to do with anything?"

I shake my head at him. Amateur. "Well, if we're at the right room," I yank the key card out of his hand and try waving it in front of the reader with no luck. "That means the data on your key card was erased."

"How is that even possible?"

"There's a reason they tell you to keep it in the sleeve." I'm always amused at how many people don't know this. It's happened to me on one occasion and that's all it took for me to remember to put in in there. At his raised eyebrows, I continue, "If you put it in with the rest of the credit cards in your wallet, it can sometimes erase the card."

"How does that even work?" He gently pulls the card from my hand, turning it back and forth. Looking for something that can explain this.

"I don't know," I shrug. "Technology magic?"

He pulls me back to him and brings his mouth to my ear. "I guess it's a good thing you came back with me after all." The way his breath tickles my ear sends tingles down my spine. I know what that mouth is capable of, and if it wasn't for this damn door, I'd be experiencing it right now. He leans back. "Seriously," he smirks, knowing damn well what he's doing, and how it affects me. "I would have been here for another thirty minutes trying to get it to work before admitting defeat."

"Well, I guess you better get your ass down to the concierge desk and get a new one."

"Why's that?" An older couple walks behind, knowing smiles gracing their face as they pass us by. No doubt thinking about what they were like when they first started dating. Or hell, maybe they still act that way. I've never seen a long-lasting relationship except my parents, and half the time they don't look like they even like each other. At least, not then. "Jolene?"

His voice breaks me out of my thoughts. "Um, because the bed is in there, and we are out here." I'm playing innocent when he knows damn well why we both want in that room.

"You mean, you want to use the bed to sleep?"

"I do like my sleep," I tap my finger against my chin. My lips curling at the game we're playing.

"Hmm, I guess I could go get a new one so you can get some sleep." He winks at me as he turns back toward the elevators. "Don't go anywhere."

Rolling my eyes, I slide down the door until my butt hits the floor. "Hurry up, tease. We'd already be in there if you listened to the clerk when they gave you the card."

"Yes, ma'am," he mock salutes and picks up his pace.

My heart soars as I watch him rush down the hallway and then disappear into the hallway. This is a playful side I'm not sure others get to see. I'm only happy he allows me in. Allows me to witness the soft side of his hard exterior.

I know I have a good ten or fifteen minutes until he comes back. I might as well do something useful.

Jolene: Hey girl, did you make it home okay?

Lana: Yep. Snug in my bed. You home?

Jolene: Nope. At the hotel with Bentley.

Lana: Why the hell are you texting me?????

Jolene: He had to get the key card reprogrammed.

Lana: That's funny. Maybe next time he'll learn.

Jolene: Maybe…

Lana: Y'all look really happy. You have a glow you haven't had in months.

Jolene: Thanks. Do you think it's too soon to be this into him?

Lana: Nope. If you're happy, run with it. You gotta do you.

The elevator door dings, and seconds later I see Bentley step into the hallway.

Jolene: Thanks. He's back, gotta go.
Lana: Have fun. ;)
Jolene: I'll catch up with you tomorrow.

Bentley nods to the phone in my hand when he reaches me. "I wasn't gone that long."

"Oh hush," I raise my hand in the air so he can pull me up. "I wanted to make sure Lana got home safely."

"And did she?" He raises an eyebrow as he pulls me up.

"Yep."

Somehow in all that he also waved the new key card in front of the door lock, and it flashes green. He turns the handle and pushes the door open. "I think we should pick up where we left off."

Bentley's arms wrapped tightly around is all the comfort I need. His breathing is soft and measured, and I'm almost certain he's asleep.

I scoot over the tiniest fraction. Just enough to get away from the insane body heat he gives off. Seriously, no person should be able to produce that much heat. I don't make it far, though. "Where are you going?" he whispers against my neck.

"You're too hot," I grumble as he pulls me even closer. "I even have my foot sticking out of the bottom of the blanket."

"Fine," he concedes. Even though it's what I wanted, I miss the contact when he scoots away from me. He might be across the bed now, but he's still on his side, and his finger runs slowly up and down my arm. The room is quiet, and soft light filters in around the curtain. "I have a question."

My eyes were drifting close until he spoke again. "What's that?" The words almost connected together.

"How do you feel about meeting my mom?"

That one small question has my eyes popping wide open. There's no way I'll fall asleep now. "Are you sure that's a good idea?" I take a deep breath. "I mean we haven't really been together that long. Isn't it a little soon?"

"I don't think it's soon at all." He scoots closer and runs his hand down my arm until his fingers are intertwined with mine. "I've already talked to my mom about you. I kind of had to after she saw the cameras focused on us." His hand squeezes mine. "I wanted to tell her sooner, but figured I should talk to you first. She's really excited to meet you."

My heart is hammering, and I'm not sure how to respond. I can't remember the last time I met someone's parents. It had to have been high school. I damn sure haven't taken anyone home to my parents considering they basically cut me out of their lives. But I wonder if he's ever taken anyone home. That's a big step, and the insecure side wants to know this. "Have you taken anyone else home to meet your family? I just don't know what to expect."

I feel bad for even asking the question. He doesn't need to justify past relationships to me. He's never asked me to do it. I told him about Carter because I wanted to. Because I needed him to know why I had the reservations I did. But he doesn't scoff. He only pulls me close to him despite my earlier complaints about him being the equivalent of a space heater. "I've never taken anyone home to meet them. I almost did once, but she proved to be someone that didn't give a damn about me. She only wanted the popularity that comes with being with one of the players on the team."

"Didn't your mom question why you never brought anyone to meet them?"

He nuzzles his chin against my shoulder and neck, and I relax in his arms. "Not really. I've always been a pretty private person. And they know that if I bring someone home...I'm serious."

Serious. That's what he means for us. He's serious about me. I should have guessed considering he's gone above and beyond what any other man has done. He didn't give up on a date with me, sets things up virtually, and he's there. Always. He's definitely shown me how serious he is about me. "Ok." I take a deep breath. "I'll meet your mom."

"And my sister," he adds.

"And your sister," I sigh. This is going to be very interesting. The worst they can do is not like me. "Now go to sleep. We have to get up early to get you to the airport."

"But I want to do other things," he pouts while his hand travels south.

"Nope. If we do that, we won't make it to the airport on time." I pull his hand back up until it's resting on my stomach. "If you don't stop, I'll go sleep on the couch."

"Yeah," he strengthens his hold on me. "That's not happening. You're not leaving my arms until you absolutely have to."

I guess there will be no space and I'll be sweaty come morning. But that's fine. At least I have these moments with him tonight.

Kisses on my neck are my alarm. Bentley pushes the hair off my face when he notices me stirring. I know it hasn't been that long since we've gone to bed, but I won't argue with how he's waking me up. Mornings aren't my thing, even when I have to go to work, but this is my own slice of paradise.

"I wish we could start the day like this every morning," he mumbles in my ear. "That's probably the best sleep I've gotten in ages and it's only better because I get to wake up next to you."

Cue the warm fuzzies. I've debated telling him I want to look for another job. Mostly because, well...we haven't been dating that long and I don't want him to think the change is because of him. I'm obviously not that sort of person. The one to derail my life for a guy. But, it's time. I'm exhausted from all the travel, and if I could find a job that doesn't require me to travel as much, then I'll be happy. With, or without, Bentley by my side. "That could be a possibility."

"What do you mean?" His lifts his head up and tilts it to the side like a confused puppy. It's as adorable when he does it as when they do. "Did you find a different job?"

"Calm down." I roll over until I'm facing him. His hair is sticking out in every direction, and I'm terrified of what mine looks like, but I don't care right now. "I've been thinking about looking for another job. As much as I love visiting new places, I'm tired all the time."

His eyes light up and the ghost of a smile crosses his lips. "Really? Have you already started looking?"

Shaking my head, I sigh. "Not yet. I want to be sure before I do anything. It's just a thought for now."

"What would you want to do?"

I shrug and the blanket covering us is pulled down just a little bit. "I don't know. I thought maybe a travel agent. I've seen so much of the world, and I think I could be great at recommending travel destinations for others. I haven't done any research into it, though."

"Take your time," he brushes his lips across his forehead. "Do what is best for you. I won't pressure you one way or another."

"That's good to know." I reach for the edge of the blanket and pull it off. His eyes go wide at my naked body, and he waggles his eyebrows. Before he has a chance to say anything at all, I put my finger against his lips. "We don't have time for that. We need to get ready. You're supposed to be at the airport in less than two hours."

Instead of waiting for a response, I slide out of bed and walk toward the bathroom. I haven't even made it to the door when he comes up behind me and sweeps me into his arms. "There's always time. And we can scrub each other down in the shower."

There's no point in arguing with him. I'll just enjoy my time with him while he's here. There's no use denying either one of us of what we want. I'll save the goodbyes when he walks to security.

TWENTY-THREE

Bentley

"Why are you rushing to the locker room?" Jordan calls
from behind me. "It's not going anywhere. It's in the same
spot it always is." He's quiet as I hurry along the hallway.
"Unless, it has to do with Jolene…" He lets the sentence trail
off. He knows damn well why I always rush to the locker
room after practices and games.

"I want to see if she has a date that she's flying here for a
couple of days. My mom has been driving me crazy trying
to pin something down." She texts or calls me every single
day lately. It's not exactly unusual for her, except her calls
never start with when do I get to meet Jolene? And now…
they do. She even has Gabby on my case. Like I can
somehow magically clear Jolene's schedule for her. It's even
trickier since we both have such insane work lives. And not
to mention she lives in a different damn state. It'd be a hell
of a lot easier if she did have a stationary job, that's for sure.

"You'll get it figured out, man." He pats my shoulder.
When the hell did he catch up to me. I know he has long

legs, but shit. That was quick. "I'm guessing things are going well with the two of you?"

"Yeah, it's going pretty good." Better than that actually. Even with the rushed phone calls between flights or after games, we manage to make time for each other. "Though I'm getting nervous."

"Why?" Ross joins the conversation. "Every time I see you two, you look pretty confident about each other."

"I don't know," I shrug as we enter the locker room. "I think this might be the real thing. I've never felt this way about anyone. I damn sure never took anyone home to meet my mom and sister."

"Your mom didn't really give you a choice since that reporter tried getting information out of you." He heads to his locker and pulls out his gym bag. "Have you heard from her again? I mean, since you shut her down at the court that day?"

"Nope," I shake my head and pull my phone out of my bag. "My agent hasn't said anything and she hasn't tried hitting me up on any of my social media. Hopefully, I won't have to deal with her again." Damn. No messages show up on my screen. She must not be off her flight yet.

"I hope so," Jordan says. "She's bad news all over. If she does come at you again. You need to call your agent or one of the managers because she will wreck your shit if she can."

"Please don't jinx me." I pick up my gym bag and throw the strap over my shoulder. I'll have to shower when I get home. It won't be weird for me to have the phone right outside of my shower there. I also don't want to get shit from the guys for doing that. "Anyway, I'll see y'all at practice tomorrow. I have to go get ready for dinner at my mom's."

"See you tomorrow," Jordan and Ross say at the same time as I walk out of the locker room.

"See ya," I call back. I hope she calls me before I have to go to my mom's. I mean, I don't technically have to go, but she likes to make sure I'm fed regularly because she doesn't trust me to take care of myself. I don't know how she thinks I made it through college. I didn't go home nearly as much as I do now, and I went to school in the next few towns over.

I open the door to my car and throw my bag inside. Damn I need a shower. It's been a while since Coach worked us so hard during practice but there are a couple of teams in the league that are catching up to us. We need to make sure we're on our game so we secure a spot in the playoffs.

Feeling like a teenager constantly checking my phone is getting old. And kind of impossible right now since I'm in the car. Either way, I wish Jolene would hurry and call me. There's no way her flight hasn't landed yet. Unless, of course, takeoff was late. Then she's stuck for a while.

I'm a little over five minutes from my mom's house when the bluetooth on my car says I have an incoming call. I don't wait for it to say who it is. Clicking the button on the steering wheel, I answer, "Hello?"

"Hey, sorry I didn't call sooner." I breathe a sigh of relief as the sound of her voice. "The flight was late, then a passenger got sick, and we had to get it cleaned up."

"That sounds like a pretty rough day." I definitely don't envy her job. There's no way I'd be able to handle someone else's vomit. I can barely handle my own. Hell, I usually go to my mom's when I'm sick so she can take care of me.

"Yeah," she breathes out. "Definitely not one of my

favorite days. I just hope whatever made the passenger sick wasn't contagious."

"I hope not." I'm getting closer and closer to my mom's house. I do not want to take the conversation inside. My mom will be lurking in corners trying to overhear the conversation. "So...have you figured out when you'll be flying back into Austin for a few days? I'm not trying to bug, but my mom is driving me insane."

Her laughter comes through the speakers loud and clear. "It looks like two weeks. Though, I'm not sure I'm ready to meet your mom. What if she doesn't like me?"

I pull into Mom's driveway and sit there. I'm not getting out of this car until I'm finished talking to Jolene. I see the curtains in the living room shift. It's not like they didn't know I was coming. This is the day I come over every week because it's the only day I know for sure I'll be in town while we're in season. "She'll like you."

"How do you know?" I hear a car door close and Lana tell someone the address to drop them off at. "Most moms, at least those in the movies, aren't crazy about their baby boys being taken from them by another woman."

I can't help the laugh that bursts out of my lips. "Are you kidding me right now? That's the craziest shit I've heard all day."

"I don't know how this works. I haven't met anyone's parents in a really long time."

Now the front door is cracking open. Gabby pokes her head through the tiny crack and then a hand motioning me to hurry up. I hold a finger up in response and she flips me off. Geez, love you too. "My mom has been asking me when I'm going to settle down for ages. You don't have anything to worry about with her." I pause for a second. "There is one thing, though."

"What's that?" There's a hint of fear in her voice, and I find it a little funny she's freaking out.

"She's incredibly nosey. She'll want your full life story and will feel no shame in prying it out of you."

A giggle comes through the speakers. "That I can handle. You do realize who my best friend is, right?"

"She didn't seem to question me too much when she was intent on setting us up." All she saw from me was a desire to go on at least one date with Jolene.

"Lana is pretty good at trusting her gut. And if her gut said you are good people, then she goes with it."

My sister opens the door all the way and starts down the sidewalk. Can't she just chill? It's not like the food is going anywhere. And Mom keeps everything warm when she's waiting on me. "I think I need to go."

"Was it something I said?"

I shake my head even though she can't see me. "No. I'm at my mom's for weekly dinner and my sister is marching to my car to tell me to hurry up."

"Why didn't you say something?"

"Because I haven't talked to you all day, and they see me all the time. It wasn't killing them to wait." She's silent for a few seconds, but I push on. "I'll call you when I get home, though. Hopefully you'll still be awake."

"Yeah, I should be. The flight schedule I have tomorrow starts later in the day."

"Okay. I'll call you as soon as I get home. Maybe we can have little fun over the phone..."

"Men," she says, exasperated. I'm almost certain she's shaking her head at the same time.

"Bye, Jolene."

She says her goodbye and I kill the engine, also ending the call. I barely have the door open and Gabby is standing right in front of the car. "It took you long enough."

"Chill, sis," I scold. "I haven't talked to Jolene all day."

"I'm sure you've talked to plenty of other girls, though." She says it like it's a fact. She doesn't know shit. I've barely talked to her about anyone for a long time because this is the kind of judgement, I get from her.

"You don't know shit, Gabby." I close my door and stomp past her. I do not need this crap from her.

I walk through the still open door and don't bother seeing if she's following. Mom is in the kitchen, and the smell of dinner is divine. If Gabby doesn't change her attitude, though, I'll walk back through the door and leave. Delicious dinner be damned. I'm not going to have her being an ass over something she has no clue about.

My mom must have heard me because she whips around from the stove. "You're here. You really need to come visit me more." She acts like I'm not over here once a week. "Where's your sister?"

I shrug. "I'm sure she'll be in soon. She told me I needed to hurry up." I peer over Mom and see the burners on the stove still going. "You aren't even done with dinner."

"You and your sister need to stop fighting, mi corazon. There will be a day when you are all you have." I hate when she talks like this. It's something she tells us every time we get into a disagreement. But we're siblings. That's what we do...we bicker and then make up.

"I know, Mom." She turns away from me and stirs the meat in the skillet. Carne Asada is one of my favorite meals, and I love when she makes it. It always gives me the peace of being home. "Do you need any help?"

"No, it's almost done." She looks over at the table and rolls her eyes. "You can set the table since your sister didn't."

We hear the door close harder than necessary and she shakes her head. As soon as she hears me get the plates down from the cupboard, she throws out her next question. "When will I get to meet this girl of yours?"

"In two weeks," I grin. It's hard not to. She'll be coming into my world for a bit. Meeting my family, and getting to know them. "She'll be in Austin for a couple of days. We can grab dinner after the game, or she can come over here the day after."

"I'll cook," she nods. I'm not arguing with her. Her food is amazing, and Jolene won't be able to eat Mexican food from a restaurant again. Not after she's had the real thing. "Get the table set, I'll bring the food over."

I do as I'm asked and soon Gabby is helping me. It's a little late now since she only has to get the silverware. But I'm not going to fight with her. A peaceful dinner is what Mom wants, and it's what I'll give her.

Mom is in the living room watching her novellas while Gabby and I clean the kitchen. Even though I kept things peaceful, you could feel the tension rolling off of my sister. I don't know what I did to piss her off, but I'm over it. She's practically slamming the dishes into the dishwasher, and I worry she's going to break something. "Dude, you need to chill. If you break one of those plates, Mom is going to freak the fuck out." My voice is a harsh whisper because I try not to cuss when I'm around my mom.

"You can buy her a new set," she snaps back.

"Not the point, Gabby," I point to the dishes in question, "those are the ones she got from Abuelita. She will lose her shit."

My sister takes a moment to think about that. Finally, something to calm her ass down. There are only a few more dishes to add to the load, and I'm done wiping everything down. This is the one time a week I really clean anything. I have a cleaning service come by my house. I've tried offering Mom the same thing, but she refuses and says she can clean her own house. Most days I wish she would let me take care of her and make her life easier, but others...I know exactly what she means. She needs to feel useful, and cleaning is her thing.

I ball up the rag in my hand and shoot it toward the sink. It goes in without ever touching the sides. "Do you always have to play around?"

"You mean have fun? Yes," I nod. "I always have to have fun. I'll be on the porch if you need anything else." Turning my back to her, I walk down the small hallway leading to the laundry room and out the back door. Mom put a table out here years ago. It's where she likes to drink her morning coffee.

I pull one of the chairs into the yard. Looking up, I study the sky. Wondering if Jolene is on any of the planes flying overhead. The stars are almost non-existent among the bright city lights. I wonder what it's like to look at the night sky without any distractions.

Lost in my thoughts, I don't realize that someone is joining me until I look over and see my sister has pulled a chair next to me. "You must really like this woman."

Seriously, that's how she wants to start this? "I wouldn't be bringing her around if I didn't. She's different than anyone I've dated before."

"You mean she doesn't want you for your success? Like those other girls you're photographed with?"

Honestly, I didn't realize she knew about them. That's

beside the point. "She's nothing like them. She's smart, funny, and she isn't scared to go toe-to-toe with me if she doesn't like something I do or say."

"You basically just described me," my sister deadpans.

"Please don't ever say that again," I shudder at the thought. "Anyway. As much as I like her, I'm constantly worried she's going to bail. Like something I say or do, is going to be the last straw for her and she'll leave...just like Dad did." I don't mention that my feelings are more than just liking her. They are quickly approaching the "L" word, and I'm not sure how I feel about that either.

"I'm going to say this as lovingly as I can. Big sister to little brother." She places her hand on my arm telling me she requires my full attention. "You have spent your entire life running from any sort of meaningful relationship. Denying yourself of any happiness because Dad left. That wasn't your fault. It wasn't mine or Mom's either. He was a selfish asshole and he doesn't deserve anymore of our thoughts or time." I open my mouth to cut her off, but she shakes her head. "I'm not done. It's time for you to grow up, and stop letting that hurt interfere with your relationships. If you keep living your life in fear of rejection, you're never going to actually live."

Huh. I've never had it put to me that way before. It makes sense, but it's easier to say I'm going to do that than it is to actually do it. "It's scary though, sis. This thing with her feels real. It feels bigger than anything I've felt before."

"Then it'll be worth the wait to see how far this goes." She glances at the watch on her wrist. I don't understand why she still wears one when we have cell phones, but whatever. "It's almost time for me to get to bed. Work comes early in the morning."

"It wouldn't have to if you and Mom would let me take care of things," I grumble.

"And we'd be miserable if you did that." She leans over to give me a hug before standing. "I'm sorry I've been so bitchy to you. It just killed me to see you going from girl to girl, and I assumed she would be just like the rest."

"She's not. In any way, shape, or form. She's just Jolene."

"Gross," she groans. "I don't know how much I like you being all romantic and stuff. It's weird." She grabs the chair she pulled over and takes it back to the porch. "Goodnight, baby bro. I can't wait to meet her."

I stay outside for a few more minutes, mulling over everything my sister said. She's right, even if I hate to admit it. I can't keep living in fear. I can't give myself over to her completely until I let go of everything I feel about my dad.

It's getting late, and I know Mom needs to get up early as well. I move the chair back and head inside. "Bye, Mom." I bend down and kiss the top of her head. "I'll see you next week."

"Bye, Mijo," she replies. She's called me that since I was a little boy. The only time it's changed is when I've pissed her off. "I love you, and let me know when you get home."

I roll my eyes. It's not that far away, but I know it'll do a lot to settle her piece of mind. "I will, I love you too."

I lock the front door behind me as I walk to my car. My hand is already in my pocket, digging out my phone. I press Jolene's number and the phone rings and rings. Then it goes to voicemail. I try again. Voicemail. Maybe her and Lana went to dinner. Or, she's in the shower or something. I fire off a text and get in the car. She can call me back if she feels like it, but I know she's exhausted.

Bentley: I tried calling, but didn't get an answer. Goodnight, Beautiful. I hope your flight tomorrow goes well. Call me when you can.

The drive home is silent. I don't even have music playing. All that occupies my thoughts is where things will go with Jolene. And how I can convince her to stick by my side

TWENTY-FOUR

Jolene

THE ALARM on my phone jolts me awake. Add to that the hotel clock and there's no going back to sleep. I don't even know what city we're in. The back to back flights have taken their toll on me.

I reach my hand over to turn both of the alarms off. It's ridiculous I have to have so many alarms but I know myself. I'm also not relying on Lana to wake up. Peering over at her bed, she's clearly still asleep. I could wake her up now. Or... I can use the time to take advantage of the shower and having first dibs. That seems like a better option. Lana has an issue with hogging all the hot water.

I tiptoe across the room to keep from disturbing my friend. The sentiment is almost fruitless because she did sleep through two alarms blaring. One day I aim to be like her. Or at least, go one night without weird dreams. I never had this problem before I started dating Bentley.

I turn the knob of the shower to hot and until steam fills the bathroom before adjusting the temperature. The dream from last night keeps mulling over in my mind. In it, I met a slew of girls who claimed to have been with Bentley before me. I remember breaking down into tears in the dream. But it seems as if the insecurities have followed me outside the subconscious. One day I won't deal with these issues.

Stepping into the shower, I let the almost too hot water wash away the remains of the dream. I think a lot of it stems from not talking before bed last night. We've talked every night since we started dating. Or, at least, as close to bedtime as possible. Last night he must have forgotten. I reach for the shampoo, and squirt a dollop in my hand before lathering it in my hair. Or, he may have tried calling after I went to bed. I didn't even think to check my phone when I woke up.

My eyes pop open at the realization and I'm seconds away from jumping out of the shower to check the phone in question. Except...shampoo drips into my eyes and they are on fucking fire. Shower revelations are always a pain in the ass. I rush to rinse the shampoo out of my hair and quickly wash my body. I should shave my legs since we typically wear skirts, but that's not important right now. As soon as my body is suds free, I step out of the shower, grab a towel from the rack and wrap it around my body. My hair is dripping down my back, but I don't care. I need to squash any fears I have about us.

He mentioned he was having dinner with his mom and sister. If they said anything, it could sway our relationship. Not that Bentley is someone who is easily swayed, but those two mean everything to him. If anyone could sway our budding relationship, it's them.

I march to the nightstand, ignore Lana's stirring body on her bed, and pick up my phone. I can't keep denying that I don't feel more for him, and this is that fear crawling out. I swipe the screen open and see a red bubble over the phone icon. It's from Bentley. He didn't leave a message, so I close the app and open the text messages.

My heart soars at the sight of his name. He must be waiting for me to call him back. I press his name, and the phone rings until the voicemail picks up. I hang up instead of leaving a message. Glancing at the time, I calculate the time difference. I'm on the east coast, so he's probably at practice right now. I know they start pretty early. I'll text him back instead.

Jolene: Sorry, I fell asleep last night. I get on a flight in a little over two hours. I'll call you after I land if I don't hear from you before. Have a great day, Hot Stuff.

Oh my gosh. I slide my hand down my face. Did I seriously just write that? This is a time that message recall would be great. Who the hell calls someone that? He's going to laugh so hard when he sees it. My insecurities are calmed down. For now. It's amazing what seeing him reach out does for me.

"Why are you half naked?" Lana grumbles from beneath her pillow. I think? "You better not have been sexting, or doing anything dirty, while you're literally next to me. That would be a whole new level of weird for you."

I grab a pillow from my bed and chuck it at her. "Don't be disgusting. There's no way in hell I'd be able to do that with you in the same room."

"You'd be surprised what people do when they think others are asleep." She pokes her head out enough to waggle her eyebrows at me.

A part of me wants to ask her what she's seen, or heard. But nope. I don't want to go down that rabbit hole, or hear all the sordid details. I'm sure she'll have zero issues doling out. "Hush and get your ass in gear." I grab the corner of her blanket on her bed, and begin pulling it off. "We have to head to the airport soon, and it takes you a long time to get ready."

"You're bossy," she pouts. Relenting she gets out of bed and slowly makes her way to the bedroom. I mean, moving inch by inch as if she has all the time in the world.

I get ready while she's in the shower. My vision keeps drifting to my phone. Willing a text from Bentley to come through. This long-distance thing is starting to wear on me. Looking into the travel agent business is going to be a top priority on my next day off. Something has to give.

Of course, we're running late. That's what happens when you let Lana get ready last. She takes her sweet ass time and then we're left scrambling to get our shit out of the hotel. I swear I could pummel her right now. I have no idea what the hell takes her so long. She doesn't even look like she's wearing makeup. I swear if we are dinged for being late, I'm going to start making her take showers at night. Or better yet...stay in my own room instead of trying to save International Airlines money.

It doesn't matter now, though. We're rushing through the airport like a couple of lunatics. Bags bouncing along behind us, and almost falling while we run to the gate we were supposed to be at twenty minutes ago. Something catches my eye as we pass the bookstore. They are in every airport across the world, but it's a magazine I see, and my eyes widen.

I stop in my tracks and Lana keeps hurrying forward. It takes her a few minutes to realize that I'm no longer with her. "Hey, what are you doing? We have somewhere to be right now." She leaves her suitcase where she was standing, because sometimes she lacks common sense, and marches over to where I'm frozen. "What is going—?" Her questions die as she sees what I'm staring at.

People push around us, trying to get to their gates. Searching for food, or just killing time before their flight. But my eyes are glued to the picture on the front of one of the trash gossip magazines. It's me. Well, I know it's me I'm sure nobody else does. It's from the game Bentley played in Missouri. The game I went to, and he pulled me out of the stands afterward. You can't see my face which is a bonus. But it doesn't stop the shock that rolls through me at the fact that I'm on the fucking cover of a tabloid. My name isn't mentioned anywhere on the cover. There's a question in bold, capital letters: **WHO IS THE MYSTERY WOMAN?**

I didn't realize that athletes ended up in these sort of publications, but I guess I shouldn't be surprised. That's not what alarms me, though. Beneath that is: **Will she be another in the long line of broken hearts?** Pictures of Bentley with other women surround the one featuring me. It's like a punch to the gut after my dreams last night.

These are pictures I've seen before. They popped up when I first started looking into who he was as a person. But seeing them altogether, and how different they are from me. I'm plain in comparison. Boring, and not who most athletes fall for. I'll never live up to those standards. I may be well traveled, but inside...I'm still that girl from the country trying to find her place in the world.

Lana steps between me and the rack of magazines, successfully breaking my line of sight. "This is trash. You know that, right? They do it to rile people up." She wraps her arm around my shoulder and pulls me toward the gate we're supposed to be at. Passengers won't be boarding for a bit, but we need to get things ready. "Don't pay any attention to it. We need to go, though."

"You're right." I take two deep breaths and let her lead me to our flight. "It's nothing. Meaningless dribble." Except, how do I know? We see each other maybe once a week or two, and other than the phone, we aren't able to communicate as much as I would like. All those insecurities I pushed down earlier come bubbling back up.

Passengers will begin boarding soon. We've finished wiping everything down and getting the snack area ready. This really is a thankless job. I don't think people realize all the crap we have to do before we even let them on the plane.

My phone vibrates in my pocket. I pull it out and see Bentley's name flash across the screen. I'm still stunned by the magazine cover I saw, and the only way I'll get answers if I answer the phone. "Hello?"

"Thank God," he breathes in relief. "Did I catch you before you take off?"

A small smile tugs at my lips. He doesn't sound like someone who is trying to hide something. "Obviously. Otherwise I wouldn't have answered the phone."

He doesn't address my smartass comment. "What did

you and Lana do last night? I tried calling but you didn't answer."

"We ordered in, and then I passed out." My voice is clipped, and I hope he can't hear it. I'm not trying to be snooty, but the images on the magazine, a real life representation of my dream, flashes across my mind.

"Well, while you're in Austin, you're going to relax. Except for when you meet my mom and sister. The rest of the time, we're going to hang out at my house, binge watch TV, and have all the crazy sex we can manage in a short amount of time."

"Mhmm," I reply. Thirty minutes ago, that would have sounded wonderful. Thirty minutes ago, I didn't see all his past conquests splattered across a glossy piece of paper.

"What's wrong?" I can't tell if he's playing dumb, or if he really doesn't know about the magazine cover. Surely that's something his agent would have clued him into.

"You haven't seen anyone else since we've been together, right?" I'll be shocked if he heard the question. It comes out barely above a whisper. My fear is fueling the question.

"Why would you even ask that?" His voice is hard. Shit, I've offended him. "I already told you that I've been one hundred percent committed to you since that first day I saw you. I don't understand what's going on."

Lana walks by me and motions for me to hurry it up. It's almost time to get the passengers on board and situated. I might as well do this now. If not, it's going to eat at me the entire flight. "There's a, um, magazine with a picture of us from the game." He says something to interrupt but I don't let him. "And surrounding it are pictures of you with a bunch of different girls. I didn't think they were recent, but

I need to know for sure. We can't keep going forward unless we are on the same page."

"So those are the games she's going to play."

That catches my attention. "Who is she?"

He sighs, and I can hear the frustration he's been holding onto. "That reporter that interviewed me after the game. Jordan said she was trouble, and this is how she's launching her attack. I wish I knew what the hell she wanted. You know, other than stirring up shit where there is none."

"Why didn't you tell me about her before?" I'm hurt he didn't divulge that information with me.

"I was hoping it would be a non-issue. And that by not giving her anything about you, she'd drop it."

"Well, thanks for that at least." He's sincere. If there's one thing I've become accustomed to, it's detecting people's bullshit. Even over the phone. "I'm sorry for coming at you. I just didn't know what the hell was going on."

"No, you're right," he concedes. "I should have told you after the crap she pulled at the game. Jordan said she latches onto up and coming rookies. If they don't give her all the information she wants, regardless, if it doesn't pertain to the game, she makes their life hell."

"And now you have a target painted on your back?" This is why I didn't want to get involved. High profile means he'll always be scrutinized. But the way he makes me feel is completely worth it. I can weather this with him.

"Basically," he sighs. "But I'll take care of it. Even if it means getting a restraining order of some sort."

"That's good to know." Lana is waving her arms in the air and signals to the first passengers coming on board. "Look, I have to go. We're boarding now. I'll call you later."

"Okay." He pauses for a second, "I hope this doesn't

change your mind about us. You are the only person I want to be with."

"I know." And I do, but it doesn't stop the fear of him throwing me aside because I'm what he wants for now. Either way, I won't count us out just yet. "Bye, Bentley."

"I'll talk to you later, Jo." He hangs up quickly, and I know it's because he's calling me by my nickname. He's never called me that before, but it warms my heart that he feels comfortable using it with me. Especially since I was so adamantly against it when we went on that first date.

All I can do now is wait and see what happens. I'm falling for him more and more. While it's terrifying, it's not nearly as scary as losing him.

TWENTY-FIVE

Bentley

THE LINE TO board the plane is crazy long. I'm antsy to be in the presence of the woman I love. Oh shit. Did I really just think that? I can't be in love with her. Not yet anyway. It's too soon. People don't fall in love that quickly, and if they do...it's destined to fail.

I can't think about that right now, though. It's been far too long since I've seen Jolene. Only being on the phone with her is so damn hard. I can't touch her or wrap her in my arms. I can't make her scream my name, or feel her nails down my back. It's just not the same. Surely it has to be bugging her as much as it is me. The next group of passengers are called and they enter the short hallway between the building and the plane. Only a few more sections until they call mine.

I make it a point to be one of the last to board. It gives me a few moments with her before I have to take my seat. It's funny. Before her, I was always in a rush to get whoever I took home with me out of the door. The sooner they were gone...the better. That's how I know it's different with Jolene. I want to prolong the time I have with her. I cherish the small moments and drag them out as long as possible.

Finally, I enter the air bridge, mere moments away from seeing her. Dragging my carryon luggage behind me, my steps are slow and measured. The passengers ahead of me pick up their pace, anxious to get decent seats, even though all the "good" ones are most likely taken. I've gotten used to taking whatever I can get as long as it means talking to Jo for a little bit longer.

She's in my sights. Dark brown hair pulled into a pony-tail and a warm smile to greet the passengers. I could never do her job. She has to be nice to people or she could get fired. All I have to do is play a good game. Before she has a chance to even say hello, I drop the handle of my suitcase and rush toward her. Pulling her into my arms, I swing her around, and smash my lips against hers. It's overkill, but I give exactly two shits about that. It's been too long since I've felt her skin against mine.

Catcalls and whistles echo throughout the cabin. She pulls away and hides her face against my chest. "I'm at work, Bentley." She lifts her head up a bit and her cheeks are bright red. Damn, I didn't mean to embarrass her. At the same time, I'm staking my claim to her and none of these single assholes better hit on her.

"Sorry," I whisper against her hair. "Actually, I take that back. I'm not sorry. It's been too long since I've held you in my arms."

"You're ridiculous," she laughs. "Go find a seat before you delay the flight."

"I'd be okay with that possibility," I pull her closer to me.

"Yeah," she snorts. "Until they take your ass off the

flight. Then you wouldn't get to see me at all."

"You have a point." I grab my suitcase and start down the aisle. "But be prepared to head straight to the hotel when we land." An older lady sitting close to us gasps in shock. Please, like she didn't also act like this with the person she loved.

Jolene doesn't respond. She stares at me and points toward one of the empty seats. I wonder if this means she won't give me a drink and snack once we take off. That kiss was totally worth getting put on the naughty list.

So much for heading straight to the hotel room. Coach called a meeting and we've been sitting here for over an hour. I'm not sure how many more times he thinks we can go over the plays. It's all going to come down to executing them, and even that depends on how good the other team is. It could honestly go either way.

"Hey," Ross leans toward me. "What are you doing after this? Want to go grab a drink?"

"Nah, I'm taking Jo to dinner. She's waiting for me in the room." I try to tune out Coach, but he keeps talking louder and louder. As if that's going to do anything. We're as ready for this game as we're going to be.

"Yeah, dinner," he winks at me. "I guess that's what you're calling it these days."

"Jackass," I mutter under my breath. "We're actually going to dinner."

"Guys," Coach's voice booms between us. Shit, I didn't even realize he moved. "Are y'all done gossiping?"

"Sure. Are we done with this meeting?" Ross fires back. That's something I would never in my wildest dreams do.

Coach is an authority figure and deserves our respect. Not to mention I'm still the new guy. If I did that shit, I'd be benched for a week.

Coach shakes his head, exasperated, and points to the door. "Y'all get out of here. Go have fun," he pauses and stares at a few of the players. "But not too much fun. We still have a game to win tomorrow."

The entire team races toward the door. Ross is hot on my heels. "Have fun on your date." He does air quotes on the last word. And while I know there will be other activities going on tonight, I am going to take her out. She's not just a piece of ass to me. She's so much more, and I hope she understands that.

"Whatever, man," I wave him away. "I'll see you in the morning."

All the other guys are clamoring to leave the hotel and I'm trying to make it to the elevators. Once we were checked in, I sent Jolene to the room so she could relax. It's the least I could do after she's been on her feet for who knows how long. And even though she seemed to act like everything was fine between us, I can't help feeling like something's different. I just hope she isn't still upset about the photos on that magazine. My past no longer matters. Not now that she's in my life.

The elevator takes ridiculously long to ascend. If I didn't know the hotel was on the newer side, I'd wonder if this thing has ever had any work done to it. Finally, the doors slide open and I hurry out of the rickety box.

I knock on the door before I wave the keycard in front of the door. I don't want to freak her out by just barging in. "Hey, Jo," I call into the almost dark room. She hasn't said anything about the nickname, or me saying it. Fingers crossed it means I have her approval.

She's not in the sitting area. I walk through the short hallway and see her lying on the bed, a book in one hand and her phone in the other. Her eyebrows are drawn down, and she's staring at the phone. Not the book. What could have gone down while I was in the meeting? Hopefully that reporter isn't doing anything else to cause problems. "Jolene."

She jumps at the sound of my voice. "Oh, hey. I didn't hear you come in." She swipes the screen of her phone, and then locks it. That's odd. "How did the meeting go?"

"Boring," I shrug. "It's nothing we didn't already know. He's just being insane with making sure we're studying the other team. As if we all aren't watching old games to familiarize ourselves with them."

"That sounds like a waste of time." She sets the book down and comes to stand next to me. A small grin on her face, even though it seems strained to me. She's just tired. That's all. "Is there anything in particular I need to wear for dinner?"

"Nope," I pull her into me. "I didn't want to go somewhere fancy. You've got to be exhausted and I'll need to get back early."

"What time is the game tomorrow?"

"Three or four? I can't remember. I only know it's an early one." I let go of her, and walk to my suitcase, grabbing some clothes out of it. "I need to take a shower and we can go after that." Normally, I'd go in what I have on, but I didn't shower before I left the house and I don't want to go anywhere in my 'flying' clothes.

"Want some company?" She asks and stalks toward me.

Her actions are the polar opposite of her expression, and I'm not sure what to do. "It's all good. I'll be quick." What the fuck? I never turn down sex, especially when it's with my feisty flight attendant. I need to sort this out. "I'll be ready to go in fifteen."

"Oh, okay," she sighs. "I'll get ready, then."

Tonight is not going how I planned at all. When did this become so confusing? My fingers are crossed that it's exhaustion and nothing that has to do with us. It seems like she's pulling away and I don't know what to do about that. Only time will tell, I guess.

We are seated at a small restaurant close to the hotel. I want to wine and dine her, but I need to keep the heavy foods to a minimum. It'll do me no good to eat so much I get sick on the court. That's definitely not going to lead us to a victory. She's free to have whatever she wants, though.

We place our order. Grilled chicken for me, and a steak for her. One of my favorite things about her is she's not scared to eat an actual meal in front of me. Most women order a salad and then look like they are hungry for the rest of the date. Jolene, on the other hand, is a person unto herself. She doesn't care what anyone thinks, especially me. Even if things feel off, at least I know she's not going to fake anything.

"Are you excited about meeting my mom?" I have to ask something because this silence is different than other times. It feels deafening instead of being a comfort. I don't under-stand what happened. She seemed happy to see me when I got on the plane, but I could be wrong.

"Yeah," she mumbles around a bite of her food. "I'm kind of nervous, but it's nothing I can't handle."

That was a very direct answer and held very little enthusiasm. I swear. It's like we've fallen into an alternate dimension or something. Things haven't been right between us since she saw the magazine cover. But surely that isn't what is bothering her. And if it was...she should feel like she can talk to me about it. At least I hope that's the case. "They're excited to meet you."

"I am, too," she replies after another bite, but she looks over my shoulder and raises her eyebrows.

"What is it?" The urge to turn around is strong, but I don't want to bring any unnecessary attention to us if I don't need to.

"There's a woman standing outside the window with a huge camera." Damn it. Not this again. "She has it pointed directly at us."

"Maybe it's an excited fan." I start to turn around. I need to see what she's so freaked out about. There's also a chance that it's that crazy ass reporter from the game in Missouri. And if it is, I need to know.

"No," Jolene stops me. "We don't need to bring any more attention than we already have."

"We can always get the rest of our stuff to go and head back to the hotel. They don't allow anyone up to the floor the players are on. Well, unless someone approves them beforehand."

"We can finish dinner. If we're going to be together, this is something I have to get used to, right?" Her voice is shaky, and I want nothing more than to pull her into a hug. To do anything that reassures her that everything is fine. She doesn't stop staring over my shoulder for another few minutes. "Okay, she's gone." The way her shoulders sag breaks me. This isn't the life she wants, and here I am dragging her into it without asking if she was okay with it.

"I'm sorry." Both of our plates are almost empty when I finally have the nerve to open my mouth.

"For what?" she sets her fork down and takes a sip of her water.

"For bringing you into this life. You asked me at the game to keep your identity on the down low, and then those damn pictures show up on the front page of a shitty magazine. And now," I wave a hand behind me toward the window. "We have people trying to encroach on our dinner plans. You didn't ask for any of this."

She takes a deep breath and reaches across the table, placing her hand on mine. "It's not ideal, but it's not all that bad either. I realized early on what dating you would mean. I just wish it wasn't at the expense of our privacy."

"It's par for the course. I'll have to ask Ross how he gets around without the media catching on. I might be able to learn a thing or two from him."

Her head bobbles up and down in agreement. "Let's get out of here. I'm ready to go to the room." Her mouth is tight even though she's smiling. This is not how I expected our weekend to go.

"That's a good idea," I agree. "What time is your flight tomorrow?"

"Early," she shrugs. "I'll probably have to head out when you wake up, maybe even before."

"Okay." I don't know what else I'm supposed to say. But everything with us felt forced tonight. Like we're going through the motions, but there's no feeling or passion behind it. Nothing like we've had before. "We'll go get some rest. If I had known, I would have ordered in."

She doesn't say anything, and we head back to the hotel. I don't see anyone with cameras as we depart the restaurant, but that doesn't necessarily mean anything. It's going to be a long night of worrying for me.

TWENTY-SIX

Jolene

"Dude," Lana scolds me as I place things into my suitcase and then take them back out. "Stop it. If you keep changing your mind, you're going to end up going naked."

"That's not even funny." What does one wear to meet parents? A dress? Dress pants? I'm completely out of my element here and worry one tiny mistake will derail everything. Sure, I acted unaffected when we were at dinner the other night, but that was me lying to myself thinking I could do this. "I have no idea what to wear or do."

Lana shakes her head at me and forces me to sit on the bed. "I'll pack for you. You have an entire weekend to yourself with your man. Meeting his family is going to be easy, I promise."

She can't promise that, though. She adapts to every situation so easily. Me? I'm awkward and abrasive. I say and do the wrong things. "That's not the only thing I'm worried about."

"If you say you're concerned about the media, I'll

pommel you. You knew what this would be like after you started researching him. You can't believe everything a gossip magazine publishes. Nine times out of ten it's complete bullshit."

"Yeah, but what about that one time?" I mumble under my breath.

"You're focusing on the wrong thing." She goes to my underwear drawer and shuffles through it until she finds something sexy and throws it in the suitcase. "I know relationships are scary. It's part of life. But he loves you." I start to interrupt, but she glares at me. "He may not have said the words yet, but I know he does. You can tell by the way he looks at you, and how protective he is. If you have any doubts, then maybe you should question why you're going to Austin in the first place."

That's the thing. I don't have any doubts when it comes to him. It's all the women that feel the need to throw themselves at him I'm not a fan of. How desperate do they have to be to do things like that? I don't get it, and I probably never will. "Because despite the distance and all the crap I've found online, I'm right on the verge of loving him."

"There's your answer," she sits next to me on the bed, packing my suitcase is abandoned for the time being. "Stop sweating the small stuff. And that's all the other crap is. Small. Stuff. Focus on you and him. Everything else will work itself out."

"I guess you're right." I know she is, but she'll get big-headed about it if I tell her she absolutely is.

"I'm always right." She squeezes me into a hug before jumping off the bed and raiding my closet. "It would probably be a lot easier on both of you if you let him mention you. Then all the other ball chasers will realize that he's off the market."

As much as I value my privacy, she might be right about that, too. I'll have to talk to him about that when I see him. It's something I've thought about but I didn't want to jump the gun in case he's not as serious about me as I am him. I don't think I have anything to worry about, though. If he wasn't serious, he wouldn't have asked me to meet his mom. Right?

"I think that might be doable." I peer into the suitcase to see what all she's thrown in there. "You know I can't wear half of that to meet his family."

"Girl, you can wear a T-shirt and jeans to meet them. I'm packing your bag for all the sexy times you're going to have in his gigantic house."

"Why do I put up with you again?" This woman has completely lost her mind.

"Because you love me, and I'm family. You have to love family."

She's not wrong. She's the only family I have since my blood relatives are assholes. "At least you know I love you."

"I'm not sure how I'm going to feel about that once you start saying it to Bentley." She puts one more item in my bag and closes the top. "Don't be surprised if I get a little jealous. I've had you to myself for so long."

"I'm more concerned with what you're going to do when I'm no longer flying."

"I guess you found a job?" That pulls some of the excitement down. I hate that she thinks I'm abandoning her, but I have to do what's best for me.

"Not yet," I sigh. "I haven't even started researching anything. They have us on so many back-to-back flights, I can barely think straight."

"I'll support you no matter what." She grabs my arms

and pulls me up from the bed. "Now, let's finish getting ready. We'll have to leave soon."

～

The phone rings and rings. Crap. Is he already at the stadium? I didn't think he had to be there for a few more hours. Just before I think it will roll over to voicemail, he answers. "Whew, I almost missed your call. Are you already on the plane?"

"Not yet," I sigh. "Lana and I are on the way, but there's traffic everywhere. I have no clue what's going on, but they need to get out of the way. We'll get in trouble if we're late again." I give Lana some major side-eye. She's the reason we're always pushing our limits. One day I'll be smart and ride on my own. I'll miss these days, though. Not flying with my best friend, or seeing her, all the time will be weird.

"That sucks," he laments. "Hopefully whatever is causing the jam clears up soon. I'm excited to see you, and so are Mom and Gabby."

Nerves creep up all over again. Meeting his family is a big deal, and even though I'm trying to push my fears down, it's hard. Lana's pep talks can only do so much. It's up to me to dispel them completely. "Yeah, I'm excited too."

"You don't have to lie. There's nothing to worry about, though. They are going to love you." He sounds so confident about it. "I have to get going soon. I have your tickets waiting for you at will call."

"Tickets?" Who else is he expecting to come?"

"I had an extra one put with yours in case Lana came to the game as well." It's so sweet that he's willing to include my best friend. "And if she can't make it, there's no harm done."

"Thanks, Bentley. It means a lot." So many people dismiss those I find valuable in my life, but he doesn't. He's willing to include Lana as much as he can. "I'll see you in a couple of hours. You know, if this damn traffic jam goes away."

"Anytime." I can hear his grin through the phone. "I'll be looking for you in the stands."

"I'll be there." I hang up the phone and lean my head against the backseat of the cab. This thing is probably disgusting, but I don't even have it in me to care. "Can I do this?"

"Look, babe," she turns in the seat until she's facing me. "I will not keep having this conversation with you. I love you, but you're torturing yourself. What did I tell you before we left?"

"Don't sweat the small stuff," I answer, monotone.

"Exactly." Her head bobs up and down. "Things will work out, and if they don't, I'll be right here." She pauses, staring out the window, "but I don't think you'll have to worry about that."

"I hope you're right." Being thrown to the side again is one of my worst fears. I never want to go through that again. Not that I can control it, but it's why I've been so careful with my heart all this time. Until I met Bentley. He turned my entire world upside down and helped me realize I want something more. I want companionship.

Traffic finally clears up, and we've made it to the airport with minutes to spare. This is way too damn close to the time we have to come in for our flight. One day Lana will get her shit together and we'll leave on time.

We're speed walking to the gate and notice the words delayed on the giant screen. You have got to be fucking kidding me. "This can't be happening," I grumble.

"It'll be fine. I'll find out how long the delay is." Lana rushes to the information desk between the two gates and speaks hurriedly to the man standing there. He tries to get a word in, and I wish I could hear what he's saying, but I'm too far away. Lana talks over him, and he backs up a step. I've never seen him before, so he must be new. He obviously doesn't know the force of nature my best friend can be. Especially when it's helping me.

Lana turns and stomps back to me. A scowl on her face. Anger is not her best look. "What's the verdict?" I ask.

"You're not going to like it," she sighs. When I don't say anything she continues, "it looks like we'll have a minimum of a two-hour delay."

My mouth drops open. Oh no, this can't be happening. I'll miss the entirety of Bentley's game. And that's if we stick to the two-hour delay. If the man upstairs is looking out for me at all, whatever is causing it will go away quickly. "I need to text Bentley to let him know." That's the only thing I can think to say, and I'm not sure he'll get the message. He usually turns his phone off when he gets to the stadium on game days.

"It's a storm in our flight path that's causing it. I'll check the weather app in that area and see what it looks like."

"Thanks." I pull out my phone, hoping this isn't a bad omen, to shoot off a text to Bentley.

Jolene: Our flight is delayed, but I'll be there as soon as I can.

Fingers crossed I can at least meet him at the stadium.

～

I glance at my watch as the passengers get off the plane. I've always been patient with people taking their time, but tonight...I need them to pick up their step and get out of here already. From what I can tell, the Rattlers should be in the third quarter. If these people hurry, I can get the plane cleaned up and grab a cab to get me there as soon as the game is over.

Before the last passenger is even all the way out the door, I turn to the attendant's station and grab the cleaning supplies. It's time to get this show on the road so I can get out of here. I'm eager to see my guy, and that's not going to happen until this thing is clean.

Heading toward the front of the plane, Lana stops me. "I've got this. You get out of here. I know you've already missed most of the game, but if you leave now, maybe you'll get to see him afterward."

"Are you sure?" She doesn't need to take on my work because I have a boyfriend. "I don't want you to bear all the responsibility of getting this done."

"I'm sure," she grins. "You being happy is the most important thing right now and cleaning up after all these people will not do that. Now, get out of here."

I throw the cleaning supplies on the nearest seat and wrap my arms around her. "You are seriously the best. I owe you big time."

"Yes, you do, and I'll cash the favor in when you least expect it." She disentangles herself from me and pushes me toward the door. "Go before I change my mind."

Without another word, I grab my suitcase from the compartment and dash through the air bridge. Looking at my watch, I see how much time I might have. Good. Enough time to change before I grab a cab. I don't want to show up in my uniform. I'm sweaty after being surrounded by so many people in an enclosed space. I rush into the closest bathroom and change. Sadly, I can't do anything about my hair. It'll just have to stay up until we get to his place. We aren't supposed to go to his mom's until tomorrow for lunch, and it's a relief I don't have to worry about my appearance too much right now. He's used to seeing me like this.

I hurry by people coming and going through the airport until I'm in the pickup area. Luckily, there's a cab waiting there, and it doesn't look like there's anyone waiting for it. I tap on the window and he waves for me to get in. I don't bother putting my suitcase in the trunk. That takes too much time and unfortunately, it's not something I have a lot of if I want to get to the stadium before he leaves.

Sliding the suitcase in before I sit down on the seat, I call out to the driver. "I need to get to the stadium."

He looks over his shoulder at me, "the game is almost over. Are you sure you don't want to go anywhere else?"

"Yes," I nod even though it's dark and I'm not sure he can see it. "I need to go wherever the players leave from."

"Ah," he shakes his head. "I'll get you there as soon as I can."

I'm not sure what his head shake was about, but I have a feeling it's not anything good. Oh well, I can't think about that. I grab my phone out of my back pocket and search for the game. Trying to see how much longer I have. There are two minutes left in the last quarter and the Rattlers are up by ten points. By the time I get there, he should be walking out.

Headlights and taillights flash by as we make our way to the stadium. Traffic isn't as heavy as I figured it would be, but I'm counting my blessings. The driver pulls around the back of the building and waits in a lengthy line of yellow cars. "We're here."

"Can I wait in here with you until they walk out? I don't know the area very well and don't want to wait out here alone."

"There are people standing around everywhere." He motions to the small groups of what I assume are fans milling around the exit. When he sees that I'm not going to budge, he sighs. "Yes, you can wait in here. But the time is still running."

"That's fine with me." I stare out the window, waiting for some sign of the players leaving. After a few minutes, they file out one by one, some of them in pairs. Even when getting bombarded by fans wanting signatures, they smile and sign whatever is handed to them. Some even taking pictures.

I see Bentley's silhouette as he walks out, and I open the car door. My heart speeds up at the sight of him. I thought this feeling would go away after two dates but hear it is, yet again.

He hasn't seen me yet and I step out of the car, ready to rush toward him. Except a woman comes out behind him and wraps herself around him. I stop in my tracks. What the fuck? A part of me wants to call out and get this crazy lady off of him, but the other part...that part wants to see what he's going to do.

Bentley stops as well. I can't tell if it's out of surprise or familiarity. I try to get a closer look without catching his attention. The woman has long blonde hair, and she turns just enough that the light shines down on her. Holy. Shit. That's the woman I saw taking photos at the restaurant. And I'm pretty sure it was the woman interviewing him after the game I went to. Why in the hell is she hanging all over Bentley?

I take a step forward and the movement catches his eye. They widen at the sight of me, but he still hasn't pushed her off of him. My heart sinks with every second he doesn't do something. He could take a step toward me and that would be enough. He hasn't though, and I don't want to stand around waiting for him to react.

I turn around and get back in the cab. Tears threaten to roll down my cheeks, but I push them back as much as I can. "Can you take me back to the airport?"

"We just left there," he argues.

"Please," my voice cracks despite trying to keep myself together.

He must hear the desperation in my voice because he pulls into traffic and we're heading back. I pull up the list of flights, looking for one that has seats available and can get me out of here as fast as possible. I don't even care where it goes, as long as it's far away from Bentley.

This is why I didn't want to get involved with him. I thought I could handle the attention he gets, but if he's not going to make it clear that he's taken, and act like it, then I don't know that I can be with him. It's Carter all over again. The only difference is, I let my guard down completely this time. The realization breaks me and I let the first of what I'm sure are many tears roll down my cheek.

TWENTY-SEVEN

Bentley

"Jolene," I yell, too late to do any good. The cab she got in is already speeding off down the road. Shit. Shit. Shit. This is not good. My brain finally gets over the shock, and I pull away from Savannah. "What the hell is wrong with you?"

She snorts. "Don't tell me you don't feel the chemistry between us." She smiles and takes a step toward me.

I back up. Jordan and Ross were right. This chick is off her rocker. "Excuse me? Where the fuck did you get that idea?"

Hurt flashes across her face. "Why else did you talk to me after the game in Missouri? Especially when there were a dozen other reporters to go to. You can't say it has nothing to do with my looks."

I'm speechless for a few moments, and that doesn't happen often. I've talked to her once. I'm not sure how she conceived this idea in her head. "Because you were the only one not in my face with a microphone."

Her head snaps back as if she was slapped. I can't

believe I'm even having to deal with this. "I assumed you were into me after making it apparent that the woman you were with was a friend. And honestly, I can do so much more for your career than she ever could. You need to be with someone that knows the business."

"You're nuts," I yell. A few of the people still hanging out after the game turn toward us, waiting to see what drama unfolds. I don't want to deal with this publicly, but it's the only way she's going to get it through her head to stay away from me. "It doesn't matter what I called her. She wasn't ready to be put in the spotlight and I was respecting that. And I know you had something to do with getting those pictures of me and her and the prior women I've been with put into that gossip magazine." I point my finger toward her without getting any closer. "I should have never given you that interview, and if you come near me, or her, again...I will file a restraining order."

"How are you going to do that?" She crosses her arms over her chest, nonchalant. "I'm part of the press. I have a right to be at the games." Is this lady serious? Being a part of the press doesn't mean you get to be an asshole. And that's what she's doing right now.

"I'm sure your bosses would think otherwise if I go to them with this stunt you pulled." My voice is low and steady, letting her know it's more than just a threat. I'll get all the other players she's harassed together so they can give their accounts. This woman isn't here for the right reasons, that much is obvious. She's only trying to catch herself a gravy train to a life she thinks she deserves. "I want you to stay far away from me, or I'll make sure those press privileges are revoked."

Instead of giving her a chance to reply, I turn toward the parking garage and rush to my car. This delusional woman has just fucked up the best thing that has happened to me. I need to fix it, and there is only one place Jolene would go.

Twenty minutes later, I'm pulling into a parking spot at the airport. I run inside, and I don't care if I look like an insane person. Most people would if they were searching for the woman they love. It's scarcer here at night than it is during the day. That should make it easy to spot Jolene, but I don't see her anywhere. Surely, she hasn't already boarded another plane and left. It's impossible, though. It's not like International Airlines only has one plane coming and going at a time. Shit.

I pull my phone out of my pocket and tap her name. Straight to voicemail. Damn it. No ring, nothing. Just her voice telling me to leave a message. My next best option is Lana. Maybe she'll answer.

I look for her contact information in my phone and send her a text. I would call her, but it's late and I don't know where or what she's doing. A part of me is hesitant to hear what she has to say. She's protective of Jolene, and I understand why, but it'd be nice to explain the situation and maybe she could help me.

While I wait, I search the flights that are going out. There isn't another one heading to Missouri until tomorrow. Hell, I don't even know if that's where she went. For all I know, she could be on a flight to California. I assume she has some perks to being a flight attendant and can ride on pretty much any plane her company owns.

My phone dings with a notification as I head to the ticket counter and I slide it open hoping it's a message from Jolene. I'd be happy to hear from Lana at this point. My heart sinks when I realize what it is. It's my reminder for the next game. The day after tomorrow. There's no way I can fly out and make it back in time. I must wait and see if I can get a hold of her. If she'll answer me at all.

Defeated, I walk out of the airport. This was supposed to be an amazing weekend. I had plans. She'd meet Mom and Gabby, and I was going to tell her I loved her. That she's it for me, but I guess I don't mean the same to her. She didn't even give me a chance.

I get in my car and head toward the only place that could bring me comfort.

It feels weird letting myself into Mom's house since I don't live here anymore. The house is dark, and I know both her and Gabby are in bed. I thought about knocking, but I didn't want to wake them. It's after midnight and they've both worked all day. I just didn't know where else to go. My house isn't an option. Not filled with its bare walls and all the preparations I made to wine and dine Jolene. It's a reminder of what I've always felt. Of what I knew my life would be like. I honestly believed all that would change with Jolene by my side, but she's not here and I can't go there.

There's an old, worn out blanket folded across the couch and I pull it off before lying down. I don't bother finding a place to plug my phone in. The odds of her calling me are slim to none. Hell, I'll be lucky if I ever hear from her again.

In all of my dating years, I've never truly felt the loss of someone you love. The only thing that comes close is when Dad bailed. When he decided we weren't enough for him anymore. It's like being punched in the gut and being told you're not worthy. Maybe I'm not. I never took relationships seriously before. I never let a woman completely turn my life upside down. I've never met a woman who'd make me question my own fears and push them down. The moment I do, she does exactly what I've always feared. Jordan was right when he told me I needed to calm my ass down when I signed on. That I needed to stay out of the eyes of the press because it's those past one-night stands that put me in this position. Well, that reporter is partially to blame as well. She definitely didn't help matters. But I should have taken precautions when the magazine showed up. I should have put a stop to it then. But I didn't take it seriously. My eyes drift close as all the ways I've fucked this up play through my mind.

"Wake up, Stupid." Those are the words I hear as a hand slaps my face harder than necessary. "I know you hear me. Open your damn eyes."

"What the fuck, Gabby?" I push her away before sitting up. "Is that how you greet all your guests?"

She shrugs and sits cross-legged on the floor beside the couch. "Only when they are uninvited. Why are you even here? Shouldn't you be home with Jolene?"

Everything that happened last night flashes through my head. Yeah, that's where I should be, but it's not because I'm an idiot. "I don't want to talk about it."

"Well, too damn bad. You don't get that choice since you snuck in here while we were sleeping and crashed on the couch." She leans back waiting for me to say something, but that's not going to happen. "Should I go wake Mom up? I'm sure she'd be interested in why you're here."

"She's not up yet?" I glance around the living room for some sign of what time it is. "What time is it?"

"I don't know. Around six or seven? I had to go to the restroom and was surprised to see you sprawled out on the couch like you used to do when we were kids. I figured I'd give you a little wake up call."

"You're an asshole," I mutter, rubbing the sleep out of my eyes. Scooting over, I make space for her on the couch. "Get off the floor."

"Only if you tell me what happened and why Jolene isn't with you." She's not going to let up. I forgot how annoying it can be around my big sister.

"Fine. If it'll make you shut up."

She gets off the floor and settles into the corner of the couch. "Okay, now talk." She pulls the blanket off of me and pulls it over herself. She's so annoying. There are many times I wish I was an only child, but then I would have been lonelier than I am now.

"I think we're broken up."

"What do you mean you think? That's something you should definitely know." Her eyes are raised waiting for me to answer. And she's right, this is something I should know. But Jolene didn't exactly give me that chance.

I tell her everything that happened last night after the game. It's painful saying it out loud, but even more painful that it's completely my fault. That I did nothing to keep it from happening. "Then she booked it. Before I had a chance to react or say anything. She jumped in a cab and split. Just like dad. No explanations and no goodbyes." Even more than that...no closure. Not knowing where we stand or what I can do to make things right is like being on a sinking ship with no life raft. I don't know what to do besides go down with it.

Before I realize what's happening my sister's fist hits my shoulder. "You're an idiot," she yells. I know she's just woken up Mom, but she doesn't care. I'll have to rehash this when she gets up, anyway.

"What did I do?" Damn, she hits hard. I don't remember her being this strong when I lived here.

"You should have pushed that crazy lady off you the moment her hands made contact with you. Not wait like a dumbass that doesn't know what's going on."

"I wasn't expecting it." I shake my head. "My brain was in shock and it took a minute to put all the pieces together."

"I swear men are stupid." Gabby says before getting up.

"Only if they don't learn from their mistakes," Mom says from the end of the hallway.

I glance in her direction. "How much of that did you hear?"

"Enough to know that you need to figure out what it is you want."

She has a point. But damn, I don't know what I should do. For now, all I can do is wait until I hear from Jolene.

"This is such bullshit." I've barely been in the game for five minutes and I'm already on the bench. I know I'm not at my best right now, but I'm not doing that bad. There's no reason to pull me out.

Ross scoots down the chairs until he's sitting next to me. "Dude, you need to chill out." He's not usually one to meddle, but we've been hanging out more since that night at the bar. He's pretty cool to hang out with. This is one of those times he needs to mind his own damn business.

"No, I need to be out on the court." I cross my arms over my chest like a petulant child. Is it bratty? Maybe, but I don't care. Not only have I not been able to get ahold of Jolene, but Lana keeps telling me she needs time. What does that even mean? How much time does one person need to decide if they are going to take a simple phone call?

"Look Bentley," Ross says as we watch our teammates pass the ball down the court and go in for a layup. "Your heart is broken, I get that, but you need to stop bringing that shit out onto the court. That is why you're sitting here and aren't out there right now. You're playing like shit and don't deny it because you know it's true."

If I wasn't worried he could kick my ass, I'd punch him right now. Not because he deserves it but because he's right and I don't want to admit it. Jolene walking out on me is fucking with my head in the worse way possible. "I don't know what to do. She's not answering my calls or my texts. How am I supposed to clear shit up with her if she won't talk to me?" During the game probably isn't the best time to talk about this, but there's only so much I can take from Mom and Gabby. A guy's perspective is what I need. I mean, it's not likely that I'll be put back in the game. At least, not until I get my head out of my ass and play like I usually do.

"What about contacting her friend?"

Another point by the Rattlers, and acid burns in my gut that I'm not out there. "She's a dead end."

He drums his fingers against his knee and doesn't take his eyes off the court. "Well, the only option you have is to talk to her in person."

"How am I supposed to do that if she's in another state?"

"You fly your broody ass up there and talk to her like a man." He shakes his head, annoyed. "If you want her bad enough, you go after her. There's no two ways about it."

That's three people who have told me the same thing. I'm almost certain if I asked Jordan for his advice, he'd tell me the same thing. Even though she won't answer my calls, I do want to be with her. I want that more than anything. Well, maybe besides my basketball career because I've busted my ass for it, but it's only complete if she's by my side. She makes me a better person.

"You might be onto something." I lean forward and rest my elbows on my knees. Wondering exactly how I will pull this off.

"So, when are you going?" I can see him out of the corner of my eye and he's sporting a shit-eating grin.

"I have to check her schedule and see when she's off." I think her next day off is during a game day, but that might work in my favor. I'll tell Coach I have family business I need to attend to and it'll prove to her she's the most important thing to me. If anything, maybe it'll help to smooth some things over with her.

"You better make it worth it."

I watch my team win by two points without my help. And I know deep in my gut that I won't be able to play my best until I have the answers I need to move forward.

TWENTY-EIGHT

Jolene

"Have you talked to him?" Lana stopped by to make sure I'm not wallowing in self-pity. She's too late, though. I've been wallowing for the past two weeks.

"No," I mutter and pull my blanket up to my shoulders. "Why should I?"

"Because you're obviously still upset over it. You haven't been to work since that night. I mean, I know you have a ton of vacation time, but this," she waves her hands around the coffee table. So, what if there are takeout dishes littering it. Most of those are new-ish. "This is ridiculous, Jolene."

Why is she being so harsh? My heart was literally thrown into a blender and pureed. This is my process. It's how I grieve the loss of what I thought I had. "I'll throw them away later. I don't feel like getting up right now."

"No," she stomps over to me and yanks the blanket off. "You are going to put them away now." She takes hold of my arm and pulls me off the couch. "Then you're going to shower because you smell horrible."

"Gee, thanks for the hygiene commentary." I love Lana dearly, but today she's working on my nerves. "But you don't get it. I thought we would be something more. Something that lasted. Except he's just like every other man... there until someone prettier comes along."

She sighs and begins picking up the old boxes. "You don't know that's what happened. You didn't even give him a chance to explain himself."

What the hell? Did she just defend him? That's not how this works. She's supposed to be the one who damns him with me, not the one who takes up for him and asks me to be reasonable. I've gone through this before with Carter. That one didn't hit me nearly as hard as Bentley. I thought we were so much more. "So, I'm the one in the wrong? He had some chick hanging all over him. He didn't push her off. Not even when he saw me." My voice rises at the end and I'm sure my neighbors think I'm losing my mind.

Lana throws away the stack of Styrofoam she has and whirls on me. "Number one, I never said he did nothing wrong. Not even when you came and stayed with me after you came back. Number two, just answer one of his phone calls. He's worried about you and you both need to get out of this limbo. Either get the closure you need or write him off."

"Wait, you've talked to him?" The betrayal that hits me in the stomach is not something I was expecting. She's not supposed to be talking to him. That's like best friend code or something.

"I haven't physically talked to him, so calm down." She pushes me toward the bathroom, trying to force me into the shower. "He texted me asking how you were, and I told him to give you time. I told you I'd be here for you no matter what. But, Jo, you've got to do something. Let him know how you're feeling or where you want to go from here because as shitty as the situation is, you both need to move on."

At least she didn't give him much information. Well, none really. I could demand to see her phone to make sure she's not lying to me, but she wouldn't have even brought it up if she was going to. I trust her more than I trust anyone else in the world, even if she is trying to make me act like an adult. I'd much rather stay in my jammies, curled up on the couch. "Fine," I pout. "I'll consider talking to him. But I'll take a shower first because you're right, I smell horrible."

She's sitting on my couch when I get out of the shower and looking at what my TV is paused on. "You're still watching his games?"

She didn't see it earlier because the screen goes dark once it's been paused for a certain amount of time. "Yeah. Just because I'm pissed at him doesn't mean I don't want to see him succeed. He's worked his entire life to be in the position he's in, and he deserves that."

"That means you still care," a knowing smile replaces her shock. "You really need to talk to him."

"I will, but tomorrow. He needs to focus on his career tonight and he hasn't even been playing that much. Right after I left, he started playing like shit and he's been on the bench a lot." I feel bad for him being in that position, but a small part of me was happy that he's as miserable as I am. Does that make me a horrible human? Maybe. That's beside the point, though. It means that he cares and hopefully knows he massively screwed up.

"Damn, that sucks." She shakes her head and moves over to make room for me. "Do you want me to stay and watch with you?"

"Not really." I sit down next to her. "I don't enjoy

having company with my misery. It's not a becoming look, as you saw when you got here."

"That's true. Please don't let it get that way again. I don't want to have to come check on you every day like my parents have to do with my grandma." She stands to leave. "But I will if I have to. I'm not going to let you go down in a pit of sadness. At least, not until you know what you're going to do when it comes to him." She leans down and gives me a hug. "Seriously, call me if you need me. I'm off for a couple of days."

"I will." She glares at me as if she doesn't believe me. Not that she has no reason to since I've avoided all phone calls for the past week, but it makes me laugh. "I promise. No more living in filth because my heart hurts."

"Yep. Or I'll kick your ass." Without another word, she walks out of my apartment. Even when she delivers those hard truths, I'm happy to have her on my side. I'm especially happy that she told me to shower because good Lord, was I gross.

All I can do now is watch the man I love on the TV screen and wish that I was there cheering him on.

The game is about ten minutes from starting. The announcers are going on and on about which teams will make it to the playoffs. They think the Rattlers are one of the teams that will make it to the championship round. That would be a dream for Bentley, but not if he doesn't get to actually play.

They are talking about his presence on the court being minimal, and I don't want to hear it. I mute the TV and rummage through my cabinets for popcorn. I could order out again, but I'm not that hungry. This will at least give me some sustenance.

While I'm waiting for the popcorn to be done, I unmute the TV. The game is about to start and I don't want to miss any part of it. As much as it hurts to watch him play, at least I get to see him. Even though I haven't talked to him since I bailed on him. I'm not sure anyone could blame me. Any girl in the same position would have likely done the same. Well, maybe not Lana. She would have marched straight up to the woman and cussed her out. I'm not as brave as her, though.

There's a knock at the door, pulling me from my thoughts. I'm not expecting anyone. Lana left twenty minutes ago, and I don't think she left anything. Maybe she ordered me dinner or something. She does whatever she can to mama me since my mother sucks. It's one of my favorite things about her. The knock comes again, and whoever it is isn't leaving. There's only two minutes until the game starts so I hurry to the door and swing it open. "Lana, you didn't have to bring—" My words die on my lips when I see that it isn't Lana in my doorway.

"What are you doing here?" I glance at the TV then back at the man who is supposed to be on it right this very second.

"I figured this was the only way you'd talk to me." Bentley's hands are in his pockets and he looks like he hasn't had a good night's rest in days. I'm not at my best either. The clothes I threw on after my shower has holes all in it from when I was in high school, and I'm sporting a worn-out pair of yoga pants. Definitely not how I want to look right now.

"But you're supposed to be at the game." I point to the TV to make my point. As if he doesn't know that he's supposed to be there.

"Yeah, but this was more important." He leans against the door frame. "As much as I want to be out there playing, I needed to come here. I needed to come to you."

Be still my beating heart. "Won't this affect your career?" Why is that all I'm focusing on? He's putting the game second to me. That is some sort of proof that I'm important to him, right?

"Probably," he shrugs. "But I've been sitting on the bench a lot lately. As much as it sucks, it gives a person plenty of time to think." He looks into the apartment then back to me. "Can we have this conversation inside? I don't mind doing it right here, but I'm not sure it's anyone else's business."

I didn't even think about that. I'm still shocked that he's here. At my apartment. Ruining whatever chance he may have as being a part of the Rattlers. "Yeah, um, come in."

He brushes past me. There's barely a few inches between us. He had room to have more distance from me, but he chose to be as close to me as possible. I'm not sure if it's because he wants to intimidate me, or he's so used to being in my space that he couldn't help it. He sits on the couch and pats the space next to him before pointing at the TV. "So, you're watching the game?"

I don't sit down. Not because I don't want to, but because I know if I do. If I get that close to him, I know I won't be able to stay mad at him. I won't give him a chance to say what he came here to say. Hell, he could be here to tell me I'm not worth all the trouble and he's giving us the closure we both need. I clear my throat and nod. "I've been keeping up."

"That's good." He doesn't elaborate, but he scoots all the way across the sofa to give me the distance that he somehow knows I need. "What's that smell?" Jesus. Did my days of not showering seep into the fabric? That's embarrassing. "Is something burning?"

That's when it finally hits me. "Shit, the popcorn." This is why I never leave it unattended. There's a delicate balance to making the perfect bag of popcorn, and I blew it the second he knocked on the door. I rush to the kitchen and pull the bag out of the microwave. The entire bottom is burned and there's no saving it. I throw it in the trash but don't bother with another bag. I don't think I could eat while I wait for Bentley to say whatever he's come here to say.

"Sorry about that," I say as I sit on the opposite end of the sofa. "You showing up kind of distracted me. So why did you come all this way?"

"To apologize," he looks down at his hands clasped together in his lap. "I should have pushed the reporter away sooner; the minute she attached herself to me, but I was in shock that she had the audacity to do it."

"I didn't hear an apology in that." It's catty of me I know, but saying he came to apologize and actually saying it are two distinct things. Seeing that woman throw herself at him destroyed me.

"You're right." He pauses for a second before lifting his head until his eyes meet mine. "I'm sorry, Jolene. I should have dealt with the situation sooner. Right after I realized she was behind the photos on the gossip magazine."

I cut in to let him know that's not the only time. "She was the woman outside the restaurant taking photos, too."

"Damn," he mutters. "I wish I would have known that. But that makes my decision to get a restraining order against her even better. She's apparently been a nuisance to a lot of the players, and after I took the steps to get an order, a lot of the other players came forward, too."

I can't believe he took that action. It makes me feel better about the whole situation, but I still have one question. "Does that mean she won't be at any of the remaining games?"

He nods and scoots closer, but not too close. There's still an entire cushion between us. "Nope. The network she worked for fired her after they found out about it. She'd been making players' lives hell. Apparently, she got into the job to find herself a player to attach to so she wouldn't have to do anything and could be a trophy wife."

"Wow. That's kind of sick if you ask me." I will never understand people that try to do shit like that. Harassing people is never the answer.

"Agreed." He continues to scoot closer. "I'm also sorry for letting my fear and pride get in the way of coming to you sooner. It took Ross telling me to get my head out of my ass before I came. And it was even more apparent that I needed to since you wouldn't return my calls or texts."

"I didn't return Lana's either." I want him to know that he wasn't the only one I was ignoring. It was everything, and I couldn't deal. "I am glad you came, though. I was going to call you tomorrow."

"That would have been a day too long. I needed to see you for myself. I needed to make sure you were okay. To tell you I love you and I'm not ready to lose you. I won't ever be ready for that."

A tear slips down my cheek. Damn it. I'm not supposed to be crying, but the wetness mirrored in his own eyes shows how much he means every single word he just said. I admitted to Lana earlier that I still care about him. He took care of the problem that caused me to run. "I love you, too. But...you have to be mindful of how you handle those things. If that means me coming out and being in the spotlight, so be it. I just can't deal with that kind of attention you get from women."

He takes a deep breath and lets it out. "I understand that. You don't have to be in the spotlight if you don't want to. And honestly, there hasn't been anyone that's tried to throw themselves at me. Most people respect others' boundaries. But that means you can't run off if you see something you don't like. Those are the times we need to be adults and have a conversation."

He said exactly what Lana told me earlier. "I know. Believe me, Lana laid into me earlier with some hard truths." I take a second to study him, to make sure he really means everything he's said. Scooting closer to him, I take his hand in mine. "I want things to work between us. I want that more than anything because if the last two weeks have shown me anything, it's that my life is damn empty without you in it. I love you and I want to be with you."

He wraps his arms around me and pulls me into his lap. "That is the best damn thing I've heard all day. Please never leave me again."

"I won't. You know, unless you give me a damn good reason to."

"I don't plan on ever doing that again." He leans in and places a kiss on my temple.

Turning my head, I capture his lips with my own. I haven't seen him in over two weeks, and I need to feel every single part of him. He is what makes me happy. He makes me feel like I have a home.

EPILOGUE

One month later

This is the game that determines everything. The one that will either have us going back home or heading to the championships. We're lucky that it's being played here in Austin. We're on our own turf and I have the best three cheerleaders in the entire stadium.

Jolene met Mom and Gabby a couple weeks ago. They love her just as I predicted. Not because she's overly sweet or anything, but because she doesn't back down. Now I have two people that are constantly challenging every word I say. I'm okay with it, though. I love that Jolene and Gabby get along. It's also scary how much alike they are and I never realized it until they were in the same room. I'm not sure what that says about me.

I glance over my shoulder and spot the both of them a few rows up from the bench. Both of them are wearing Rattler jerseys. Jolene has the one I bought her when we first started dating and my sister has Jordan's jersey. I think she does it to get under my skin. She has one of mine but refuses to wear it. So much for sibling solidarity. Mom is up in the box with Vanessa because she doesn't like how crazy the fans can get sometimes. And because Vanessa is amazing, she is sitting up there with her.

Coach is rotating another batch of players. He isn't happy that I missed one of the games and made me sit a couple out as punishment. But he knows we need players on the court for this one. It's the last playoff game, and he doesn't want any of us getting over-tired.

The people filling the seats are going wild. Noisemakers accompany their shouts as they cheer us on. There's five minutes left in the game, and we've been basket for basket throughout most of it. We'll get ahead for a bit and then fall behind. Both of our teams want this more than anything.

I watch my teammates go from goal to goal. Making shots and defending the basket. All of us on the bench in suspense with every steal. I want this game to go on for a while. While I don't enjoy the stress it brings on, it means more time with Jolene here in Austin. She's still flying, but Gabby is helping her look for jobs at travel agencies here. I hope they find something soon because I miss falling asleep with her in my arms. I miss her being the first thing I see when I open my eyes in the morning. I could easily take care of her until she finds another job, but she refuses to let me. She's so damn stubborn, but I wouldn't have her any other way.

"Bentley," Ross elbows me in the side. "Coach is calling for you."

There's less than a minute left in the game and he chooses now to put me in? I'm not complaining. I'm lucky to be playing at all. I jump out of my chair and hurry to Coach.

"We need you to go out there right now and keep the

ball away from them as much as possible. If it ties, make sure you're the last one with the ball and you hit a three. We're counting on you, Kid."

I hate when he calls me that. I'm not that much younger than most of the guys on the team. "Got it." I go to the score table to check in. In the time it took for Coach to talk to me, the clock has dwindled down to ten seconds. It's not a bad thing. The last minute of the game can take a good twenty minutes. I will do my best to shut that shit down. We don't need overtime tonight. We need a solid victory.

The ref calls me in and Jordan passes by me on the way to the sideline. "Show 'em what you're made of. It's your time to shine."

I nod and take my position. The whistle blows and the other team throws the ball in. The point fakes me and goes in for a layup. We're tied and there's five seconds left of the game. James grabs the ball and throws it to me. My eyes are focused on the timer. I need it to get down to less than a second before I make the shot.

The rest of my teammates block anyone that gets close to me. I pass the half-court line and work my way down the court until I'm deep in the three-point zone. The clock gets to one second and I dribble the ball, line my shot up, and release the ball.

One of the players on the opposing team tries to block it but jumps too soon. His hand an inch past the trajectory of the shot. The ball swooshes through the net as the buzzer goes off. Holy shit. We did it.

"Ladies and Gentleman, the Austin Rattlers are going to the championship." The announcer yells over the speakers and the crowd goes insane. This is what we've been working toward. We still have to prove ourselves in the last seven games, but for now, we'll bask in the glory of being division champions.

My teammates rush off the bench and huddle around me. "We're going to the finals, baby," Ross hollers over everyone.

After a few minutes of celebration, I turn my attention to the stand. To the woman who unknowingly has been a part of this journey. Who gave me the added confidence I needed. She's on her feet clapping and yelling with my sister.

Making my way through my teammates, I march to the stands. It's almost exactly what happened a few months ago. She rushes down the remaining steps and flies into my arms. This time, we don't care who catches the moment on camera or what anyone has to say about it. "You did it," she screams to be heard over the fans still celebrating our win. She plants her lips on mine and clings to me. "Let's go home. I have a victory gift for you," she winks before sliding out of my grasp.

That's what she is to me. Home. She's my safe space and I'm the same for her. I didn't trust anyone, and she didn't trust men in general. But we healed each other in the best way possible. I can't wait to see what prize she has for me.

BOOKS BY CHC AUTHORS

Want to keep up with all of the new releases in Vi Keeland and Penelope Ward's Cocky Hero Club world? Make sure you sign up for the official Cocky Hero Club newsletter for all the latest on our upcoming books:

https://www.subscribepage.com/CockyHeroClub

Check out other books in the Cocky Hero Club series:
http://www.cockyheroclub.com

ABOUT KATRINA MARIE

Katrina Marie lives in the Dallas area with her husband, two children, and fur baby. She is a lover of all things geeky. When she's not writing you can find her at her children's sporting events, or curled up reading a book.

katrinamarieauthor.com

BOOKS BY KATRINA MARIE

Taking Chances
Welcome to Your Life
Cruel and Beautiful World
Ways to Go
Remember That Night
My Only Wish is You
From This Moment
Shoot Down the Stars
Love Will Save Your Soul

Cousins Gone
Gone Country
Gone Nerdy
Gone Again (coming soon)

Silverwood Bulldogs
Baseball & Broadway

Printed in Great Britain
by Amazon